USO:
Unidentified Submerged Object
By
John E. Parnell

ISBN 978-1625123923

TABLE OF CONTENTS

THE CALLING

The episode begins with a scene of teens (MABEL, CHARLIE, and JOHN) diving off near the coastal city of Eastport, Maine. They notice something moving strangely effortlessly through the water. Their report makes the news as an Unidentified Submerged Object (USO) citing.

Tony is approached by the military to examine the alien to find a way to kill the species. When he sees how the military interrogated the alien, it infuriates him.

Tony is faced with the decision to help the military or save the alien population.

Tony accepts what he feels is the calling to preserve life, though the odds are against him.

THE TRAINING

The nation is reacting to the fear of the unknown with chaos, while Tony is in his lab trying to understand the alien's biology from a sample of hair he got.

The military is setting up defenses to protect coastal cities and monitoring systems to detect alien Unidentified Submerged Objects.

Tony discovers where the aliens are living. His daughter's friend's mother (ELEANOR) leads him to a world under the sea.

THE BATTLE

Armed military monitor everything, work places, the grocery stores, hospitals and especially coastal towns.

A secret agent finds out where the aliens are living, and the plans for battle began. They also find out that Tony is associated with them.

The Navy is set up on water and underwater to fight. The aliens fight back with weapons they created to disintegrate the military weaponry. Alien homes underwater are being destroyed left and right. They had to call for help from an alien friend from outer space.

THE TRIUMPH

Tony is injecting the aliens with a substance that will camouflage the alien's blood to appear human so that they are not caught and killed.

The alien's friend from outer space showed up and the tide turns overwhelmingly in the favor of the aliens.

Tony negotiates with the military captain on a deal so the killing of aliens will not be the policy of the military. Aliens present their proposal. The proposal is accepted. The negotiations make the news, and the aliens live in harmony with earth-kind.

Novels authored or co-authored by John E. Parnell

THE CALLING

Episode 1: Aliens Among Us

The episode begins with a scene of teens (MABEL, CHARLIE, and JOHN) diving off near the coastal city of Eastport, Maine. They notice something moving strangely effortlessly through the water. Their report makes the news as an Unidentified Submerged Object (USO) citing.

A cool air was moving across the beach like a friendly wave. However there seemed to be a mysterious energy in the air itself that day. The coastline was laid almost in a fashion of common courtesy along the pathway of the winding highway. The scenic view for a drive was beautiful to say the least. Eastport, Maine was one of those places you could lose yourself in, and totally forget the outside world. Even if Eastport itself was where you just happened to live, it had that effect on people, very relaxing. It was a peaceful place where friends could go for a drive, and put their troubles behind them.

Three friends hopped in a car to take a drive to a place along the ocean that they frequented for fishing and perhaps some swimming later. Driving that day was John. He was 18, the responsible one of the three who was hoping to ride far in life on a football scholarship that was offered to him. He was a bit of a pretty boy who was at times worried about his image. He could not help but to have a complete utter loyalty to two of his best friends since he first came to Eastport when he was just five years old.

John's father was in the Coast Guard and that's what originally brought him and his family to the area when he was little. And there was also Mabel, who was 17, a self-proclaimed tomboy. She had more courage and gall running through her veins than her two friends, she had aspirations of being a professional diver. Before the three friends had hung out, she was always the one doing the things to grab attention, or to even make John and Charlie wonder if she had gone and lost her mind altogether.

And lastly there was Charlie. He would overthink everything. Neurotic to the core this one was, always checking and double checking to make certain everything was safe, certain, and exact. Charlie never really aspired to do anything in life other than learn and soak in knowledge. People would ask him where he put it all, and why he was always asking questions. He was very curious, but never the one to just dive into the water so to speak, that was Mabel's job. So, in a way, the three friends balanced each other out, according to their personalities, life experiences thus far, and the manner in which they carried themselves.

As the car edged around the curve of the highway, a strange green light emerged from the deep blue sea. It caught Charlie's attention. Without looking away, he poked Mabel's arm, she was listening to her music on her mp3 player.

"What is it Charlie?" exclaimed Mabel with annoyance.

He was silent. He pointed out to the water.

"I don't know what that could be, but it's something extraordinary. What could do such a thing?" Charlie said.

John was totally zoned out of the conversation that Mabel and Charlie were having. He was too busy concentrating on the road to worry about what they were looking it. For all he knew, they could be staring at some fancy kid's balloon on the water that just happened to look strange or weird. Things like that happen from time to time. The best explanation for something like that was the tourists which roll through town inflating things and even forgetting them, sometimes those things are exotic by design. And later, people might say it's something more than what it really is, thus blowing the whole situation out of proportion.

Charlie and Mabel were both quiet in the back seat of the convertible. Their eyes were fixed on the object that seemed to effortlessly stream along at an amazing speed under and through the water.

"Could it be a fish?" Charlie asked Mabel.

She was silent and shrugged her shoulders. She had since removed her mp3 earbuds. Charlie reached into his backpack.

"What are you doing?" Mabel asked Charlie.

"I always record the strange things I encounter in life," Charlie replied.

Mabel said with a chuckle, "Do you plan on writing a book some day?"

Charlie sort of just glanced over at her. The thought had not even occurred to him. Of all the things that he thinks and daydreams about, and much less worries about, he never thought about writing a book based on his thoughts and of the weird life experiences that he has recorded. Charlie was busy writing away, looking at his watch, checking the wind speed, the temperature, every single small detail about the day. He also was noting who he was with, their reactions, and what exactly they were doing precisely in this possible strange moment in their lives.

Charlie and Mabel watched the water attentively. It's as if the green light was matching the speed of the car, but at the same time continuing to move smoothly and effortlessly through the water. The green light was becoming brighter and brighter as if it were getting closer to the surface. Whatever this thing was, it was also getting closer to the shoreline itself as well.

It was approaching shallow water, and thus it was poking up out of the water just enough to see an odd shape protruding upwards. It looked like an emerald but circular in shape. The green light was becoming the brightest it has been yet. The strangest part about all of this was the fact that there was no sound other than the movement of the water.

Charlie was squinting as if looking for who could be driving the contraption. His eyes were peeled to his binoculars.

"This can't be real. It just can't be," Charlie said.

He was completely drawn into the wonders of what they were experiencing. Brief shadows could be seen as his eyes scanned the large green top of the item in question that was for the most part submerged under the water. He tried to think of every possible rational explanation.

"Maybe it's tourists trying out a new rich toy, or perhaps it's an actual visual anomaly, like swamp gas that is natural but believed usually to be something that is out of this world." No, he thought, that just can't be. "It's beyond human understanding and everything scientific that I know to be true."

Everything that Charlie had ever learned in school, had ever read in books, and had listened to in church was now being called into question by what he is witnessing before his very eyes. He was both terrified, and extremely excited that they were seeing something that most people go their entire lives without ever getting such a chance to witness this phenomenon. For a moment, he thought a wild and crazy thought, "maybe I am hallucinating all of this, maybe it's all just in my head." Those thoughts were quickly walked back across the bridge they ran over in his mind, especially with the look that was in Mabel's eyes, he knew that she felt it too, the terror, the excitement. She was wondering everything he was at the exact same time.

A weird static sound began to come over the radio. It was a cross between a squeaking and a horn-like sound, as well as a hollow yet distant vibrating pitch. Another way that the sound could be best described was that it seemed very similar to the "sounds" that NASA had recorded in space that planets were giving off.

John tapped on the radio.

"Crazy thing. What gives? What's wrong with this?" John complained.

The song on the radio kept going in and out as if something was interrupting the frequency of the radio station. All of the electrical components in the vehicle slowly began to malfunction, even Mabel's mp3 player. It's as if something just squeezed all of the power out of everything electrical in the car. The timing could not have been worse. They had been driving up a large hill and had just reached the other side. And knowing John, he usually rides the brakes to play it safe. The last thing he wanted to do was piss his old man off by wrecking his beloved convertible.

Charlie and Mabel's eyes were snatched away from the water as they began to ask John.

"What the hell are you doing?"

John replied in sheer terror, "All the power's gone. I don't know what happened. The car just shut off."

He tried to restart the car, and even pump the gas petal. Nothing. The car raced down the hill, faster and faster. It reached the curve with a fury. John tried to turn the wheel to somehow slow the car down and prevent it from going off the fifty-foot drop off, and thus landing them all in watery graves on top of the rocks far below.

Charlie and Mabel were screaming at the top of their lungs. John closed his eyes and muttered prayers from his lips, hoping and praying for a higher power to somehow intervene. Up to this point, John had not been paying attention to the item in question that was roaming through the water as if full of its own intelligent will. Just as the car is about to be thrust over the side into the water, it finally reaches about twenty feet from the edge of the metal guard rail. The functionality of the brakes had resumed and the car made an extremely loud screeching noise, coming to a complete halt right in front of the green mile marker number nine sign. Smoke filled the air around the car, as did loose gravel. Black lines of burnt rubber were all set in perfectly jagged lines behind the car. The trail led all the way back up the hill. The smell of the rubber was thick in their noses, as was the fear in their hearts, and tears in their eyes. None of them wanted to say it, but they were all thinking the same thing.

"What just happened?" John finally said.

Charlie and Mabel looked at each other. Mabel was staring off into the air fluttering her lips. Her thoughts were racing, trying to figure things out. Charlie was writing as fast as he possibly could. Tears filled Mabel's eyes as she realized that she actually almost died. The red convertible came to rest at a place in the road where the ocean was not visible if you looked out over the other side of the road. The left side of the road was higher, meaning the right side of the road dipped down.

The radio was still halfway working at this point, going between an odd crackle and a gyrating twisting sound with a humming thrown in. Bits and pieces of an old blues song that did not belong on the selected modern rock station played over the radio. It was quite a spooky moment. John was looking around, wondering what the hell was happening. His eyes were filled with just as much fear, if not more than his two best friends. He looked back and up at Charlie with his binoculars on intensely staring at something out in the water. At the moment John seemed more worried about the wellbeing of his friends, especially Mabel because of how she was reacting. He was not even thinking about what Charlie was looking at.

John looked over at Mabel, her eyes were red and filled with tears. She could not bring herself to say what she saw. Mabel was visibly shaken, and crying uncontrollably. John tried to calm her down and console her.

"What's wrong? What did you see?"

All she does is point a single, small shaking lone finger out towards the ocean. Her mouth opened, attempting to say something, but she was so utterly filled with terror, whole words could not come out. She stuttered.

"Look!" she finally said with reluctance.

Charlie was still standing up in the back of the car, glancing out over the water watching the object which sat there as if it was a wolf protecting his pack. Charlie had locked in and had since stopped with whatever emotional outburst that he had been experiencing. John unlocked the door. He pulled the handle towards himself to open it. A loud click sounds and then noisy springs. This did not help the tension filled situation. "Crunk!" He pushed the door of the driver's side of the convertible open slowly. John stood up, walking closer to the edge until he finally saw it. The object out in the water that both Charlie and Mabel had been so focused on. It was green, glowing and was like nothing that John had ever seen before in his entire life. He did remember hearing his father speak of such things growing up, things that were witnessed out on Navy ships, but sailors and other military crew were ordered to keep their mouths shut about said sightings. John's eyes got big as if they were witnessing what his dad and his crew might have seen over the years in the same area.

John looked out at the unbelievable sight that was sitting in the water. It's almost like they were being watched just as keenly as they were watching this big green object in the water. It kept hovering up and down, all the while making waves in the water. Charlie could see figures walking along some panel within this ship, or whatever it may be. John reached up and snatched the binoculars out of Charlie's hands.

"Hey, I was looking at that!" Charlie loudly complained.

The binoculars were pressed tightly against John's face as if he was a ship's captain looking to go to war. The entire time, both Mabel and Charlie were trying to take pictures with Charlie's camera and an mp3 player that had a camera. The electronic equipment was halfway working at best. Pictures full of noise, static interference came out, one picture among dozens of attempts each.

"This is odd. My iPod won't take any pictures," Mabel said.

"And mine won't take any either. I am not having much luck either. You saw what it did to the car. We almost ended up in the water no thanks to our star quarterback of a driver."

"It's some sort of electronic device or possibly an electromagnetic interference," Charlie said.

John looked away slowly, with hesitation, at Charlie. Even though John already knows the answer, he wanted to hear the reassurance of the guy who is always the smartest in the room. Charlie is that guy.

"Well, Charlie what do you think?" John asked.

John stared up at Charlie, and Charlie stared out at the object, all while he had been busy at writing more descriptive notes down.

"It's an Un …"

Before Charlie could finish what he was going to say, the object went back underwater and shot off quickly away from them at an incredible rate of speed.

The three friends were looking out in awe into the sea. What a beautiful sunny day it had been, which was intended for fun, fishing and swimming. It had just become a bit gloomier. The mood in the car had changed. They made it to their destination. Charlie was more worried about writing down every single small detail that he could remember, the shape and possible size of the aircraft that they saw in the water which burst away from them underwater, like a racing missile. John and Mabel tried to fish and get what they had seen off their minds, but the silence between the three of them said more than any words could possibly convey. After they ate the picnic food that they had packed, it was not long before they decided to call it a day.

During the ride back home, the silence continued. Mabel turned on the radio to break the dull air. She was still too nervous to use her mp3 player because it had scary static images come across the screen while they were trying to take pictures and record the object. The radio seemed to still be affected. The modern rock station was still crossing over with the old blues rock station. Mabel seemed satisfied with it none the less, but John reached his hand over and turned the radio off without even glancing at Mabel. John was still clearly shaken to his core.

One by one, he quickly told them, "Tell no one what you saw here today. Keep it quiet. We don't need attention." His two friends agreed. John dropped them off one at a time.

When John pulls into the driveway of his house, he's sort of scared. He sees his dad's blue truck.

"He's never home his early," he thought.

Before he could get out of the convertible, his father had already slammed the screen door behind him. The look on his face could only be read as blank, stern, and a lesson was about to be learned. His father approaches the car, leans down putting his hands on the driver's side slot where the power windows rise from.

"Do you have any idea what you have just been implicated in?" his father asked angrily.

The star quarterback's hands were still on the steering wheel. John was sweating bullets when his eyes glared over to his father.

"Those two so called best friends you've known since you were little, they have run their mouths to the local news channel and the local newspaper. This could destroy your chances at that full ride scholarship. The media has been calling the house because your name has been included with all of this as a witness to the sighting of an unidentified submerged object. They want to interview you," his father continued angrily.

His father looked at him. His eyes were like daggers piercing into his soul.

"You will do one interview. This is what you will say, 'My two friends are crazy and under stress from school', you will not add your eyewitness description to theirs, however you will deliver said disinformation. And if you don't, I will make damn sure that scholarship goes goodbye forever, and you will be working on the deck of the ship with me before you know it, where you belong. I will make your life a living hell boy. Also, you will confiscate any and all writings, pictures, and evidence of any sort, that your so-called friends collected. And you will end your friendships with those two. If you do not comply, my promise will be delivered regarding the rest of your life," his father said.

Within moments, John pulled out of the driveway. Going to the houses of Mabel and Charlie one at a time telling them everything that his dad said. So, the three came up with a plan. Copies of all the evidence would be made, and would be given to his father, and he would sell a lie to him, so that they could go on television to tell their story. John brought the copied evidence and the iPod back to his father who was very pleased with his son. John was in tears. His father had a huge smile on his face, thanking John for his dedication to National Security.

"I can't believe you made me do this. I'm gonna go for a drive. I'll be back later tonight," John said in a distraught voice. But in reality, he was putting an act on for his father. He was heading over to pick up Mabel and Charlie.

That night on the 10 o'clock news on both *Quoddy TV* and *Gen-oTV* which service Eastport, the big story was about the sighting of an Unidentified Submerged Object, out near the highway that runs along that beach at mile marker nine in Eastport, Maine. John's father sat in his reclining chair with a thick sweat on his forehead and arms as he watched the interview of his son John and his two best friends, Mabel and Charlie as they were questioned about what they saw. All of their evidence was put on display, during the hour-long special interview for all the viewing public to see. Copies of the information were also made available on the TV station's website, and circulated through the local newspapers: *The Quoddy Tide*, *The Machias Valley News Observer*, *The Calais Advertiser*, and *The Bangor Daily News*.

For a brief moment the incident, known as the "Mile Marker Nine Sighting, in Eastport, Maine," made the national news. John's father sat there, uneasily wondering about the aftermath of the situation. He was wondering out there just who was watching, and what was going through their heads about what had just aired. One thing was for sure, John's friends meant more to him than a full ride football scholarship. The three friends stood there and witnessed the unthinkable after nearly dying. It changed their lives forever. And there was no way in hell, they would ever part ways as less than friends. In a way, it made them all closer, like family.

Episode 2: The Interrogation Room

Tony is approached by the military to examine the alien to find a way to kill the species. When he sees how the military interrogated the alien, it infuriates him.

The following day after the late-night Television interview and the newspaper article things seem to quiet down. Sure, there's been an escalation in tourism and even some news van's and federal blacked out vehicles making their presence known but the town still seems to have its overall peaceful essence. Tony opens his eyes. The clock says 4:59 am. He barely slept a wink of sleep last night. There's so much going through his mind. Will men in black show up to make him and his son, as well as his friends, disappear? Tony is well aware of the WHY of being quiet in these situations, it's exactly why he threatened to have his son's football scholarship taken away. After he realized there was no chance in hell of getting any more sleep, he got up, showered, and got read for the day. The black coffee pot was calling his name, his eyes were burning and heavy, it was only now that he was feeling regretful for not trying harder to rest and get good sleep. There was just too much running around in his head. Tony walked outside to fetch his newspaper which was rolled up tight in a plastic bag per usual, nothing out of the ordinary, other than it felt a bit heavier than normal. He looked around. Carefully slipping the newspaper from the plastic sleeve, a tiny yellow manila envelope. It felt like something hard and rectangular was inside. The tall man in Navy slacks opened the envelope and down rolled a burner cell phone. The creepy part, was when it rolled down into his palm, it actually began to ring. Tony looked around as if he felt he was being watched, he saw no one. Little did he know however the scope of a very distant sniper, had eyes on him, in case his response is not the desired one. Meaning they were gauging his reaction to the conversation. Another man in the same vicinity of the sniper held a cell phone to his ear, and some glasses that allowed him to see things over a thousand yards away with a clear picture. Tony's heart felt as if it was trying to crawl out of his chest cavity, he was impaled with

17

fear. The phone was flip open phone that was ringing very loudly in his hand.

He could feel the red dot on his forehead. He knew if he did not answer he may end up in another state as a john doe somewhere, with a brand new cold fitted toe tag. He immediately flipped the phone open. The sweat rolled down his face as if there were no tomorrow.

On the other end of the line, a man in a voice that was disguised as some deep digital replacement simply said to him, "Will you be at the far side of the park on the other side of town at 9 pm? say yes, you don't want your head splattered on that nice beautiful lawn of yours. Also sit on the bench that is near the nice trees."

The man on the phone went a step further, "buy some new damn lawn furniture. Those green goblins look like the enemy."

The other end goes dead. A sizzling sound emits from the burner phone, and it actually begins to self-destruct and Tony throws it, the phone explodes. Never in all his years in the United States Coast Guard has he had an encounter like this. Well, he has had to speak to officers with the Office of Coast Guard Recon, concerning certain investigations, centered around sailor sightings on the ships that he had been stationed on. Tony has never been contacted by any sort of black ops types, for clandestine situations. He was about to go on a terrifying journey. The day breezes by with his sailors performing their daily duties, not knowing what's in store for their Senior Chief later that evening. Their lives were carefree, his was about to become more complicated. Not only is Tony a Senior Chief Petty Officer in the Coast Guard, is also a certified marine biology scientist, he has made a living in the Coast Guard of helping study strange undersea life. He has even written a few research papers for the Coast Guard, which has at times drawn the attention of the higher ups. As Tony watches the sun escape the horizon on the ship that is docked, it's almost as if he feels his life possibly slipping away at the hands of some mad man waiting for him in the dark.

He feels the eyes upon him as he takes his briefcase and walks towards his truck. The whole ride to the park, his nerves begin to become extremely unsettled. Tony pulls up stops, and he approaches the area of the park the farthest side near the bench and trees that he was told to go towards and wait at around 9 pm, it's a bit after nine. Tony feel's a presence approach him, the footsteps get closer, he's expecting two cold rounds in the head, after everything that has happened.

"You're late," says a deep echoing voice to Tony.

He attempts to turn around.

"Stay as you are, says the deep voice, call me Craig."

"What do you want?" asks Tony.

"What we want and what we need are two different things, what we did not want was your loud-mouthed son and his friends running their mouths on television in that interview, they caused a commotion for us, a problem. What we need from you is your cooperation, your help."

Tony thinks to himself for a moment, "What could I possibly help you all with?"

The figure dressed in blacked out attire, that included a black mask to conceal his face.

"We need you to examine something for us, to find possible weaknesses," said the deep voice.

"What do you need me to examine?" said Tony.

The man in the black attire, was still, with no answer. He simply hands a folder to Tony.

"Go here at this time and wait, you will know what it is when you see it."

The dark figure gave Tony directions and a map, but to what? There's also a small envelope with papers in it. It says, "Do not open until asked."

"When do I go to this place?" Tony asks the dark figure.

"Tomorrow, same time, but to that place," says the figure. And just like that, the man in black attire disappeared off into the night.

Tony's heart the entire time was beating a thousand miles a minute. He hopped in the truck headed home and fought and kicked to try to get sleep, he knew the next day would bring interesting yet apprehensive things.

The next morning Tony woke up, went through his normal routine with no problem. He arrived at the ship for the normal run through with the crew. His cell phone rings at his side. It's his son, John, and he's quite upset.

"Dad, they've arrested us. You need to come bail us out," cried John.

"Wait, hold on, calm down. Who's arrested you for what?" his father said with an angry voice.

"All I know is they are Feds. They are dressed in black. They won't say, they got me, Mabel, and Charlie. They took Charlie up to some observation room I know not why. His girlfriend Charlotte was freaking out about the arrest. It all happened right in front of the school when we were getting out for the day. It embarrassed the hell out of us, making a huge scene."

Tony rushed to the area where they were being held. His heart jumps as if it's trying to crawl out of the side of his mouth. He only glanced at them for a moment, but the roads that he's driving down, and odd directions that John gave him sounded vaguely familiar. When he arrived at the place they were being held, he took out the map to look at the address and directions. And it turned out to be the exact same place that he had to be at 9 pm later that night.

Tony walked into the office that had a door which looked as if it belongs on a submarine. He could not find a keyhole. There was a black pad with a large clear flat LCD screen. For some reason, he had the gut feeling of pressing his hand against the flat screen. A laser wiped across his hand. A digital voice, started speaking.

"Please open the envelope and insert your card."

"This is too damn weird," added Tony. He opened the envelope slipping the card out and swiped it, on a small card device that came from nowhere above the hand screen.

The door opened and cool air rushed out. It seemed like they had the atmosphere of the enclosed location set to be a particular variance.

Tony thought, "I wonder what the hell is being stored in here, such pressure above ground like this?"

He walked in and the odd submarine door closed automatically behind him. A voice, the deep voice from the other night, invited him to head towards Interrogation Room 5.

Tony walks towards the room. He is told to watch. Some being is on the other side of the glass being poked, prodded, and treated like a wild animal. Someone is also asking it questions.

"What are you doing?" asked Tony in an annoyed tone of voice.

"Relax they are the enemy. We're just trying to find out what makes them tick. We need to know what all of their weaknesses are, in case we face them in a battlefield scenario," said the dark figure with the deep voice.

A simple knock is heard on the door, and the dark figure reacts.

"My work is done here. I will let the Captain assume command of the operation."

A tall well built, muscular man walks in. He has a thick handle bar mustache and his hair is buzzed off to a fine thin layering. He looks like a jarhead. The man stands there for a moment, as if trying to size up Tony.

He squints and reaches his hand out towards him, "Captain Peter McGurk of the Weapons Division, and you are?"

Tony walks up to the man, out of respect, even though he is annoyed by the situation at hand. He reaches his hand out to shake his hand.

"Senior Chief Tony Cheverie, glad to be a service in the situation."

Even though Tony honestly did not like what was going on nor did he want to be there, he sure as hell did not like it that his son and his friends were picked up and were being questioned.

"Did the previous whoever that was brief you on this?" asked Tony.

"Brief me?" said Peter.

He laughed, "He is a black ops liaison that works for me."

The level of fear felt as if it was spiking in the room. He'd never felt more uncomfortable in a US Navy uniform than he did now, especially with everything that's happened today.

Tony watches on as an alien creature is practically tortured. They zap it with electronic instruments. And they were using any and every possible poison or non-lethal weapon possible to test the effects. From there they were testing lethal weaponry on it. The screams that left its mouth were so horrid that Tony had to walk out of the room. He took a step away, and felt a hand on his shoulder. It was Captain McGurk.

"Soldier, you're gonna wanna stay for this. It's fixing to get icky."

All of the safety protocols were being removed with the tests. The alien was going to be given the full test treatment.

Tony became worried, "Won't that kill it?"

"That's the point," replied McGurk.

The more that Tony watches, the more it angers him. He clinched his teeth with pressure, grinding up in his fists. He could not take an innocent creature being tortured. Now if they were on the battlefield and the enemy was armed, the situation would be different, but this is a creature not from this world that is being tortured all in the name of quasi-science. And with the knowledge that Tony knows as far as being a Marine Biology Field Scientist for the US Coast Guard, this "interrogation", is completely nonsense.

Tony finally walks out of the room down the hall in disgust. The sounds of the alien in pain echo through the corridor a bit. McGurk follows him out not long after.

"And yeah, how about that, we picked up your boy and his buddies. At first, they were not cooperative. But for some time now, at least since we threatened them, they have not shut up," added McGurk."

Tony glanced over at the Captain and scoffed, "What more could they possibly tell you?"

"Well, the young man Charlie who witnessed what was going on with the USO, and took excellent detailed notes of the incident, something has happened with him. Ever since we brought him into the building, it's as if he's been channeling this thing that we are interrogating. He is proving to be a possible future asset for our program, but with the way he is currently helping us, he's gonna fit in here nicely."

Tony walked into the room that Charlie was sitting in. He was sitting at a table, eating a meal, with a drink and with a notebook. Basically, they were catering to Charlie, and he was milking that cow for all that it was worth.

Boy could that kid eat. "I have not seen you eat this much since last year's Super Bowl Charlie," joked Tony.

Tony sat down and patted him on the back, making sure that he was being treated well.

"How are things going so far?" asked Tony.

"Things are great Mr. Cheverie. Are John and Mabel doing alright?"

"Yes, they are fine," replied Tony.

Even though he has not spoken with them yet, he felt the best thing to do was to lie to the young man. He was being used, but it would seem that he would end up helping the cause somehow.

McGurk picks up the notebook that Charlie's been writing in. He shakes his head.

"Truly amazing stuff."

The Captain hands Tony the notebook.

"Here, give this a read."

The information within its pages consist of everything from the history of the aliens and their dying home world to more information about traveling the galaxy and the universe. There's even a section about Time Travel. McGurk's eyes swell up, as he realized how sensitive the information was. He had to call in an NSA official, so that the sensitive National Security documents could be secured properly. So, while the Captain was on a secured phone call with an NSA official, Tony went into detail with Charlie.

"You can't let them keep you here kiddo. You and the others, you all have lives, you know."

Charlie looked up at Tony, "Yeah I know."

Charlie suddenly began to panic, "Omg, omg, what time is it?"

"It's 7 pm Charlie why?" replied Tony.

"I had a date with my girlfriend Charlotte. We were supposed to go bowling, then to the movies. She's gonna kill me. She'll think that I stood her up," added Charlie.

"I'm sure that she'll understand Charlie. I mean John did say that you all were picked up in front of the school. Just call her when you get out of here, but do not mention anything that went on here what so ever," added Tony.

"Sounds good Mr. Cheverie. I miss my Charlotte. I should have never agreed to go to the lake with the gang."

Charlie sat there with his hands in his lap, shaking his head in worry as if he knew how truly deep down the rabbit's hole he knew that he would be going. Without warning it happens again, this time in front of McGurk and Tony. Charlie stiffens up, his eyes roll into the back of his head. McGurk motions to an assistant for a fresh note-book and black ink pen. Charlie's hands are already shaking as if something is trying to get out. The young man begins to speak in a language that is not known to the planet, and he begins to write more. The information they gather now seems to be something along the lines of plans for invading planets, at least that's what they think it is, but that's not what it is. It's really plans for how to turn a planet that will not support life, into one that will. A digital recorder captures Charlie's intense channeling.

"We'll analyze that later," adds McGurk.

Before Tony leaves he tells the Captain that before he leaves, he wants the three kids to be signed into his custody. McGurk gets in his face. This is the first real sign that from this point forward, these two men even though they are on the right side, they will not be getting along, at all.

"Well, then that's nice and fine and all. You just make sure those three kiddos don't go loud mouthing what they have seen, heard or experienced here, because if they do …"

At this point McGurk makes a childish sound effect with his mouth, conveying the picture that somebody will receive bodily harm or worse if they talk.

Tony replies, "They understand, and I will be responsible for them."

Tony leaves the room while Charlie is still channeling and writing and speaking in the odd language. He visits his son, John, who has been sitting quietly. It would seem that the event that occurred effected each youth in a unique way. Charlie, it opened him up to a talent that he never realized that he had. John, it's as if someone turned on a switch and he began to care more intensely about people than ever before. And Mabel, she was not so much fearless anymore. She questioned everything, and she did not seem to be so much of the one after attention anymore either.

Tony walked into the room that John was in. John rushed over and hugged his dad.

"I'm sorry dad. I should have listened. I didn't know. I am so sorry. I love you dad!" added John in calm yet strong tears."

"How's Mabel?" asked Tony.

"Not well. She's very shaken up, not herself at all. Dad whatever happened, whatever we experienced, it's done something to us. I can feel it. It would seem that Charlie is more affected though," added John.

"I know. I went and saw him first," added Tony.

"What are you going to do?" asked John.

"I'm getting you guys out of here. They want Charlie to stay on permanently, but he's a kid that would have to be his choice."

Before Tony can even get the rest of his words out, his son says something shocking.

"Dad I think we should stay here and help them, especially Charlie," added John.

"Well son, that's up to him, and nobody but him. We can't make him do that," added Tony.

There is a knock on the door. The door barely cracks open and an aroma of hot pizza ebbs its way through the flow of the air in the room.

John smiles, "What I got hungry. It's not easy work being a government USO witness."

The military officer hands the food and drinks to John and he begins to chow down.

"I'm starving." John dived deep into his meal.

Tony could not help but be worried. He walked back through the hallway. McGurk had walked back into the room with Charlie and came out infuriated. He slammed the door behind him, yelling obscenities.

Tony looks over to McGurk seeming amused by his angry reaction.

26

"Won't talk?" asks Tony.

With an obnoxious attitude, McGurk replies, "He has come across something that is an extraordinary discovery to say the least, but he has stopped. He won't help us anymore until we bring his high school girlfriend Charlotte up here. He won't say another word or help any more until we bring her up here. He's even asked for a private escorted date for both of them, with all expenses paid to a local bowling alley of their choice in the area, all to themselves, reserved for a day, with no questions asked. Oh, and he wants the same thing done at a movie theatre of their choice in the area, with whatever movie they want. What's next, a damn mall?"

Tony laughs. "Young love. What can I say? We all were once young, Captain. They are kids being kids. Let them be kids. And I'd do what Charlie asks. If I know him right, he will not help you if you don't do kind things in return for him. Now if you do all of that, he may be the best employee that you've ever had in this place, whatever this place happens to be," adds Tony.

McGurk replies, "This is a secure off the books, black ops facility, of course in cooperation with the US Navy. And every three-letter agency that comes to mind."

Episode 3: Judgement

Tony is faced with the decision to help the military or save the alien population.

After Charlie and Charlotte had the wishes for their all expenses date fulfilled.

Charlie begins to show as well as tell Captain McGurk everything that he had been withholding during the remote viewing and channeling sessions. Charlie covered everything from who the aliens were, where they were from, what their biological weaknesses were and why they were really here.

The Captain did not care either way. His orders were to derive the information and to figure out how to either control or destroy them all. The information could very well turn the tide in a war against these creatures, thus stopping them in their tracks without any hesitation from humanity. Even though their mission may be one of peace, the powers that be want war. They do not trust their visitors from outer space. Regardless, they see them as a foreign threat of unbelievable circumstances.

The next day Tony receives a phone call.

"Senior Chief Cheverie, you are needed back at the operations outpost for a briefing," says a command assistant.

Following his assignments that day, Tony makes his way to the operations outpost. He walks through the same old submarine looking door after putting his special card into the slot.

Tony is not exactly sure what room he's supposed to go to. He receives a text on his phone from a private number.

"Conference room at end of hall."

He continues down the hall peering into the rooms that have all of the lights out with the exception of a light or two hovering over what seems to be scientific examination or surgical tools. Tony reaches the conference room following a lengthy walk. The door

29

opens inwards to an awaiting Captain McGurk. His hand is reached out towards Tony with a smile. The smile only a mother could love and only a fellow military man could distrust. Tony knew that this man was up to no good. He had a deep feeling in his gut that the man could not be trusted. Nonetheless, he reached forward to shake McGurk's hand.

"Glad to see that you are being a team player after the interrogations, and that you are fully onboard," added McGurk.

"Anything that I can do to help with this cause, I am there," replied Tony.

The Captain invites Tony into the conference room. The lights are turned out and they begin to watch the highlights of the remote viewing sessions with Charlie.

"This boy is amazing," says McGurk. Tony looks at McGurk with a sense of worry in the dark as they watch the classified film.

"Charlie is going to be a great asset to us. I've already been ordered to have him assigned a special clandestine detail of his own."

Tony nearly chokes on his coffee.

"You're going to have a CIA handler assigned to this kid?" says Tony with some shock.

"It's classified. It will be a three-letter agency I have been told, but I was told it's being kept anonymous for National Security reasons," added McGurk, "however I do think he's going to get a CIA handler. That's what they do in situations like this."

And thus more shock.

"They?" asks Tony.

"The group in D.C. in charge of all operational data concerning this subject. They have been around since the days of Roswell. They were our predecessors. If it was not for them, this entire thing would have gotten out of control a long time ago. They put specific controls in place to make certain the public did not lose its lunch, that John and Mary Q taxpayer went on about their business all while we were being visited by little green men. And yes, since you are major part of this thing now, you are officially in the pay grade. You are in the need to know. From now on, just like me you will receive daily briefings."

Tony is handed another cell phone.

"This line is secure. It's made from sophisticated technology shared by a little green friend. If you are not within simple travelling vicinity of a proper meeting location, then use this phone and you will receive your daily briefing. I believe that you know that line is not to be shared or made known to any other person, nor said briefings. It is classified to the highest clearance levels. So basically, if you get a call from the President asking questions about little green men and being curious, I want you to start talking goofy marine lingo about the dolphins in the area. Not a word about the little green men. It's above his paygrade as well. We get all of that from time to time. We've had a few people in the past attempt to break said protocol. They were made examples of."

Tony inspects the phone and puts it his pocket. The film ends and the lights are turned on. McGurk hands Tony a folder. Tony flips through it, it's everything from pictures about the underwater USO's, to autopsy pictures from the past.

"These may be helpful, it's a bit of a mixture of information. There's also a personal copy of the remote viewing with Charlie so that you can apply said intelligence along with everything you know about. The ultimate goal is make a weapon that will destroy them."

Tony looks down at the disc, the pictures, and the files.

"It's all like a giant jigsaw puzzle in a way," adds Tony.

The Captain looks at him amusement.

"Well, it's just a large amount of sensitive information that if looked at correctly and deciphered in the right manner, you can find a way."

"A way to what?" asks Tony.

"Control and or kill them," adds McGurk.

At this point, McGurk is sold on Tony. Tony has been given a sensitive security clearance to accomplish this mission, to do a job that he is clearly seen as an expert at being able to do, studying odd marine life. And figuring out their weakness or how to use them.

"Are we all good here Chief?" asks McGurk.

In between the questions McGurk is asking, time almost seems to slow down. Tony's hearing rate rises. Sweat thickens on his skin. His fear response doubles. He is both angry and scared because of everything he saw the other day. And he realizes now what he must do. As a human being and a scientist, not just a Naval Officer. The ticking clock on the wall even seems to stop just for him so he can ponder everything that's being asked of him. It's almost like the world is being put on hold for this lone decision. Stand with the military to destroy the little green men, or help the aliens who are seemingly coming here in peace and to help us. Back to reality Tony bursts.

"Are you on board with helping use destroy this threat?" adds McGurk.

Tony smiles and shakes McGurk's hand.

"Consider it done Sir, you won't regret this," adds Tony.

And just like that, Tony has just convinced his Commanding Officer, Captain McGurk, that he's on born with the destruction of a peaceful alien race. In reality, his aim is to use the intelligence to help the little green men in any way that he can. Tony gets up and walks out with the sensitive documents, pictures and the disc with Charlie's full remote viewing session on it. He goes home, locks himself in his study and encloses himself with all of the material. It honestly takes a few hours for everything to hit him. The shock of the situation, the fact that he has received the highest possible clearance known to exist within the United States Government. And that he is being trusted with sensitive classified information regarding USO's, aliens, remote viewing, and all the witness testimony to go along with it. The emotions hit him, and he swells up with an empty and horrible feeling inside. He's being asked to go against everything he believes in, which is the peaceful preservation of life, whether human or another form of animal or marine life. A huge dilemma weighs over his head now, to help the government take said information derived from Charlie's remote viewing sessions to use against the aliens to destroy them, or to somehow use said information to help the aliens in any way possible. Tony makes an attempt to find a way from every possible angle to perform the military operation but at the same time somehow saving the alien species. At this point he believes he makes a breakthrough, but then he realizes that it won't work, because every single variable in the operation is known by the government.

For hours, Tony is hold up in his room. John brings his friends Mabel, and Charlie over who are wondering and worried about what has Mr. Cheverie hold up in his room for so long. At this point the kids are very concerned. They don't know what to think. Tony tried to weigh the pro's and con's of every decision. Whether it was helping the military and eradicating a peaceful alien species, or helping the aliens and if it were to destroy mankind and the aftermath. And there was always the thought that they were actually telling the truth and that the information found in the remote viewing sessions was one hundred percent accurate. Tony could hear the kids beating on the door wondering what was going on. He could sense the worry in their voices. They were a part of this now. The government was using them like guinea pigs and did not know it, yet they seemed to be alright with it.

"If only these kids knew the entire situation, and what the government was planning," thought Tony.

He felt as if he was going around in circles with this decision, and coming back to the same dead end plan. He was so tempted to tell the kids, but he was afraid that Charlie would accidentally spill the beans in a remote viewing session.

So, it was then and there, that he took the files, pictures, the disc all into the living room. All three of the teenagers were sitting there. You could hear an ink pen drop in the room.

They stared at Mr. Cheverie not knowing what to think.

"You okay Mr. Cheverie?" asked Mabel.

Tony just looked back at the teenage girl with an unsure look in his eyes. You could see the formulation of tear droplets within his eyes. The look in his eyes, his bloodshot colored eyes, were of a man who had been up for many hours. And he had been exposed to things he never thought he would see in his waking life. These things had also appeared in his dreams at night as well, making him question absolutely everything he's ever known and done in his own life. It left him wondering, "why, what's the reason for it all?" Tony was looking for answers and he was about to find them.

Tony stood in front of the kids with the classified folder in one hand and the disc containing Charlie's remote viewing session in the other hand, and other uncut material that was recorded that day.

"What's all of that Dad?" asked John.

"The key to everything, absolutely everything," replied his father.

Tony makes direct contact with the three youngsters.

"Whether you realize it or not, the three of you went through a life changing event the other day. Making your appearance on the news may not have been the smartest thing ever, because you got the attention of some people who run in some very dark circles within the United States Government," says Tony.

The kids seemed to want to add their own two cents in, but they seemed unsure of how to react to Mr. Cheverie and his suddenly open behavior about everything he'd wanted them to be quiet about before. Tony points to Charlie.

"Your friend is the key. If not for what he has seen, then this would not be possible. None of it,", added Tony.

"What do you mean Dad?" asked John.

His father responded, "Charlie has an ability that apparently he's never known about. It's quite possible that the slightly traumatic experience that you all went through at the same time with the Unidentified Submerged Object incident at Mile Marker number 9, did something to him. It brought something out within him that had been held perhaps dormant all of his life."

"But what?" asked Mabel.

"Charlie is some sort of psychic. That's the best way to say it," added Tony.

The three kids began to laugh.

"Charlie you do remember the sessions with McGurk right?" asked Tony.

"McGurk? Are you okay Mr. Cheverie?" asked Charlie.

Then it hit Tony like a ringing bell. He wondered if McGurk did something to the three teenagers while they were at the classified black operations facility. Tony did not want to think that the Captain would stoop so low to erase any previous short term memories of the three teenagers.

But now, Mr. Cheverie was seriously considering this possibility. He flipped through the file again. Information about the entire Mile Marker number 9 incident was there as well as well as pictures of the three kids, and their debriefing testimony that was taken at the facility, in full detail. Of course, the full remote viewing sessions were there as well.

"Don't you guys remember anything?" asked Tony.

He knew what he had to do. The silent response from the kids said it all, something was done to them at the facility without them knowing it. Tony basically believes they were given a retroactive drug to erase certain memories. It's the most logical explanation for their not remembering the Mile Marker number 9 incident, much less not being able to remember being at the operations facility the other day.

"So none of you have any weird memories over the past few days of going anywhere with me?" asks Tony.

The kids laugh.

"No sir, no dad," reply the kids.

"What is this all about dad? did we do something wrong?" asked John with worry filled laughter.

He does not respond to John's silly question. He has a serious look on his face that turns towards his own anxious worries.

The three teens look at each other and John nods his head.

"Dad look, Mr. McGurk pulled all three of us aside and wanted us to not talk to you about any of this any further."

"Why not?" asked his father.

"We don't know. All I know is each one of us was given something that we asked for. Me a better football scholarship opportunity than what you were gonna take away from me, as well as something about helping me get drafted into the NFL," added John.

Mabel seemed a bit embarrassed about what she wanted. The usual center of attention that she used to be, she had become more much reserved after the incident.

"I asked for a way to get my mother out of jail sooner. I miss her. And for a job within the government someday, something that involves science," added Mabel.

"Charlie, asked for a full ride scholarship to Harvard, no questions asked. He asked the same for Charlotte. And to be able to treat Charlotte to a date anytime he wished as long as it did not interfere with any of his work. In return, basically the government wanted him to not just be a remote view and channel for them at times, but they wanted Charlie to become a full-time intelligence analyst," added John.

"Mr. Cheverie he did not give us any retroactive drugs to erase our memories. We were promised things and in return told to not speak to you any further about any of this," said Charlie.

Tony's heart pace quickens. He steps closer to Charlie and looks at Mabel and John.

"Did you just--- did you just read my mind?" asked Tony.

"I'm sorry Mr. Cheverie I can't help it. It's like I hear all of these random whispers of words after the incident. Some things are gibberish, other things can be explained away without effort. Just like I know that you are having a dilemma about telling us many things right now that are on this disc you want us to watch," added Charlie.

"So you are not only apparently able to remote view, you can channel nearly anyone or anything, but you are a telepath as well. You can read minds. Do you have any idea what they are going to do to you?" asked Tony.

The three teens hated breaking their promise to Mr. McGurk, concerning not speaking to Tony any further about anything having to do with the USO's or their eyewitness encounter.

Tony began to realize that the reason behind that may have been that the Captain wanted to keep the teens at odds against Tony to prevent any sort of mutiny situation from occurring. McGurk did not like the television interviews, but why have the black vehicles show up at the teen's school in broad daylight breaking protocol? wondered Tony. Apparently, McGurk wanted to show that he was in charge. Tony figured that the Captain is the type of man who goes on power trips. People like that can't be trusted they are destructive individuals. The Chief opened up the folder and brushed through it. He stared down at the Disc, and back at the kids, making direct eye contact with Charlie. There was information in the files and on the disc that the teens did not know about, well except for Charlie. He knew bits and pieces but not the whole picture. The information about the goal of the military to ultimately destroy the aliens and all angles of the public relations cover up attempts and the plans to follow afterwards. He has a tough decision, to keep them in the dark about his own thoughts and feelings or tell them everything. The phone rings, it's his daughter, Jenny. She was letting her dad know that she would be home from college for summer break soon. She was bringing her friend Eleanor with her for undisclosed reasons, but the they would be there soon. Jenny and her friend Eleanor sounded excited about something, but would not lead on to what said thing was. Randomly, Charlie smirked and giggled, whispering under his breath, "Maybe they can help us."

Tony said his goodbyes etc. to his daughter telling her to be very careful on her journey home. Jenny is John's older sister, by about four years. He hangs the phone up and takes a deep breath.

"Guy's what you all are about to see and hear on this disc, are things that happened at the facility you were at, but also things that were said and happened that you do not know about," added Tony.

"Just show us and tell us Mr. Cheverie. It's okay. John and Mabel don't know, but I do, well at least some," said Charlie.

Yes, Charlie was holding back a lot, and Charlie knew way more than he let on. One thing is for sure, Tony was right about Charlie being the secret weapon.

Episode 4: Tony's Calling

Tony accepts what he feels is the calling to preserve life, though the odds are against him.

The tight knit group of teen's John, Mabel, and Charlie sat and watched the DVD of the interrogation, along with all of the comments about them that were being made. Charlie watched on even though he already knew everything. The other teens were at a loss for words. Everything felt so unbelievable and surreal, especially with the alien autopsy footage that was going on just doors down from where they were being interrogated.

The deals thrown their way to hush them into working for McGurk. Even though the promises were legit, the premise of everything was just so wrong.

After watching the film over and over, Tony sat with the kids talking about everything from what has been on his mind to all that had happened the day before with meeting the dark figure in the park. Charlie already knew all of this, because he heard Mr. Cheverie pacing in the room and his thoughts were ringing out loud like an audio tape recording playing back words. That night, Tony told the kids to go home and some spend time with their families. That what came next would not be easy on anyone, but that they would be there for each other no matter what and they would do the right thing no matter what.

Father and son sat on the porch in the rocking chairs that were gifts to Tony from his father and mother. It was three, maybe four hours in the dark, and likely close to midnight. Sounds from the lake that lie merely yards from there house gave off delicious splashing sounds from all of the fish that normally bite at that time of night. Frogs were erupting with ribbits from all over the body of water. A white, yet shining moon gleamed overhead it looked so steady and big, almost ready to hit the earth. It's as if someone placed it perfectly in the sky like a centerpiece for this world. The cool breeze danced and made a lovely song with the wind chimes on Tony's front porch. He lived in a two-level ranch style house with his son. There was a spare room made up for his daughter Jenny as well, but she'd been off to college for some time now. The quiet sound of the lack of any words was a welcome one for Tony's ears especially with all of the crazy things that had happened within the last few weeks, not to mention the past few days. He'd barely had any sleep to speak of. His eyes had grown heavy and well streaked with red from having had only three hours of sleep in two days. Mr. Cheverie could barely move. He breathed in and enjoyed the still of the night, the song that the water was playing quite peacefully. It made him think about this whole thing between helping the military destroy the aliens and the preservation of life. It's at this exact moment that Tony was wishing that Charlie was here, to explain things much better. He was having a bit of a tough time getting the words out the way that he wanted to.

"Dad, they're monsters. We can't help McGurk. He will kill them all," John said. When John's calm words broke the hours long silence, Tony was a bit disappointed. He actually did not want to talk about any of it. For a while he wanted to pretend that nothing else mattered in the world, but this perfectly quiet and peaceful moment of father and son sitting on their front porch and just spending quality time together.

John continued, "They will wipe them all out." His emotions got the best of him. "We can't let that happen Dad!"

Tony was still quiet and rocking at a slow pace. He was breathing calmly and still his eyes were heavier than ever. He had his hands folded on his lap like a retired old man.

John became so upset about everything that he fell to his knees on the porch and began to weep more. This actually got his father's attention, waking him up. Tony watched on realizing the great pain and fear that his son was in. He'd already decided what his course of action was. To use the military intelligence against the military to help the aliens survive, instead of helping the military kill the aliens. Mr. Cheverie looked down into his hands that were scarred by many years of hard work and middle age. They were the hands of a hard-working family man who just happened to be in the military and have a Top-Secret security clearance. He pulled a folder from the side of his chair and opened it. He saw pictures of the alien's body parts, close up photos of its hand. It had four fingers, compared to Tony's five. John was still on his knees crying and Tony was looking at the pictures of the alien's hand and his hand side by side. Seeing these things angered Tony and made him emotional, but the tears had not fully simmered to the surface yet.

It was at this moment that Tony had thoughts of his grandfather, who raised Tony for the most part. His father, Terry, was always off on some mission with the military. Both of the men were always getting into it. He'd always put the military ahead of family and life in general seemed like such a nonchalant situation to him. Tony's grandfather, Tom Cheverie, would tell Terry how important the sanctity of life was. Terry would ignore him and get mad at Tom when he'd tell Tony these things. He did not want Tony to grow up being a weak-minded fool with a feeble heart. Tom told Tony nevertheless, how important life itself was, even those of our enemies. That it was the last stronghold of mankind, that our hearts and minds were the one thing that the enemy could never attain. That even though we may hate one another, or dislike each other, deep down we were all brothers, with similar blood running through our veins. We may not all look the same, but we were made by the same creator. His grandfather would point to his heart and towards the sky when saying this. And there was never a day in his life that his grandfather was without his handy Bible. Tom went on to tell Tony that their will was unbreakable, and that hope was our greatest weapon, though some would argue otherwise. His grandfather shook them off as naysayers.

"Don't you ever let anyone tell you different. You heard it here first," his grandfather used to always say. His father Terry was one of those naysayers. Tom had just enough time with Tony growing up to instill in him the proper tools and values that he would come to need one day.

Even when the day came that Tony's grandfather passed on, and he had to deal with his father, he'd already come of age and become able and ready to handle anything his father could throw at him. It was as if his father did not want to believe that life could prevail, and that evil was not absolute and infinite. Tom always tried to make Tony understand that there was good in this world, in men's hearts, even his own fathers heart, but he was too afraid to let his guard down to see that good. That his father was afraid of the unknown. Tony was not. Sitting in the chair looking at the pictures, thinking about all of these things from his past. All while his son was sobbing on the front porch deck, Tony had fully accepted what he felt his calling to be. To preserve any and all life at any cost. Tony would not let the aliens perish. He was going to do anything and everything in his power to ensure their survival. He felt that letting them die would be a great sin against the morals that his grandfather had raised him by. Mr. Cheverie no longer saw them as aliens, but purely as living creatures just like humans. They lived, breathed, ate, and above all, they felt emotions, they loved. It was so obvious of such a thing in the interrogation room when the special operations officers were harassing the alien and scaring it. That was one of the many things that irked Tony, but at the same time he realized, if they can feel fear, then obviously they can feel other emotions. Tony had realized that they could love as well. He was overwhelmed by the moment. The tears fluttered down Tony's cheeks. He could not control them any longer. They had been years in the making, all of the good tears and the bad tears. Everything from all of the life lessons learned from his grandfather Tom, and quality time they spent together, to the hate-filled arguments with his father after Tom passed. Tony felt it all. He had not wept in years. The outpouring of his emotion, after he had been quiet for so many hours, caught the attention of his son John. John looked over at his father's direction in the dark.

He saw his head in his hands as he wept over the pile of pictures, both from the alien information folder and from old family photos. By this time, John's tears were still a few and mostly drying up, his nose had been swollen with mucus from all of the pouting. His eyes were red from being so upset. The young star quarterback walked towards his father in the dark slowly, placing his hand on his shoulder.

"Dad I'm sorry. Is there anything that I can do?" John asked.

His father looked up at him, realizing that he had instilled the same values within his son that his grandfather Tom had instilled within him. Tony, even though he had a great task ahead of him, knew that he had always been doing the right thing in life with his kids, making sure that they grew up the way his grandfather taught them, to respect, preserve and most importantly protect life.

Tony cleared up his tears.

"I am so proud that you are my son, and how you turned out to be. There is nothing anyone could give me in this world that would ever make me want to change that. You and your sister are the best things that ever happened to me," added Mr. Cheverie.

As Tony hugged John and embraced him tightly, everything felt like it was coming full circle. It was everything. Protecting the aliens, preventing death and destruction on epic levels of horror and terrible pause. All while protecting his family and friends, along with respecting the values and ideals he was raised with. Mr. Cheverie knew everything he had to do, and exactly why to do it. He also felt an intense dread with the entire situation. From this day forth he would feel it more so every time he goes to the Special Operations station. He would go in, do his job, get intelligence and return home to analyze and determine his next best course of action to help the aliens preserve life. He knew however that he had to put on an act, and that in certain places he would have to give just enough to the military information wise to appease them. In fact, Tony would dribble it like a fine-toothed comb. He would even have to play dumb at times. The full scope of just how difficult everything would be, had not hit him until now. How much he had to lie, that's something he's had to do in the military more and more when it came to anything having to do with National Security or protecting the sanctity of life. All these years, his grandfather's words still rang true in his head like a morning alarm clock attached to his heart and soul.

Even though he dreaded returning to the facility, he knew he had to. It was his duty to do so, he knew that he was the only military person there who would give the aliens, much less his family a fighting chance. This was what his grandfather raised him for, to be, to assert onto the world, hope. An everlasting love and life, for, above and by humanity, whether they chose to believe or even feel it.

Just as much as Tony was dreading returning to the facility he was also relishing his chance to make things right.

He wanted peace between the alien race and humanity most of all. Before he kept thinking about it and it bothered him more and more. But now, the more he thought, and kept the mindset that his hopeful mindset, the more he believed it could be done. And every single time he had the slightest doubt, he heard his grandfather's voice, encouraging him telling him that he was doing the right thing, and to never let anyone tell him different. Those words put his mind at ease, that no matter how hard it would get, how tough or danger-ous, as long as he was alive, he would see his family through this. That as long as there was life in his aging bones, that the aliens had a fighting chance at peace with humanity.

Tony's values and ideals were the reason he went into marine bi-ology in the first place when he went to college and then joined the United States Coast Guard. He had a desire to go fight and kill. He wanted to serve his country all while protecting the common good. At the same time. Whether good or bad, through fear and courage, Tony knew the danger of double crossing the United States Govern-ment, its military and even said covert special operations programs. His life and his family's lives would be in danger, but he had a plan in place that if anything went wrong that they would leave and start over, that he would stay and face the consequences, thus sacrificing his own life so that they could live on peacefully. Tony had bug out bags with papers ready for them He just hoped that it never came to that. He was trying to think as many steps ahead of McGurk, the mil-itary and the government as possible. The last thing he wants to do is to tip his hand to show that he wants to support the aliens and go against the military and government. All of which meant every time Tony went back to the facility, he would have to develop this persona of wanting to kill them all. He'd thought about it before, but he real-ized more and more just how much actual acting he would have to do to make McGurk believe him, even though he could not stand the ground that McGurk walked on. The guy was a dirt bag in Tony's book.

When Tony and John finally released their embrace both of them, father and son. Knew what was ahead. They both locked up the house for the night turning in and shutting the lights out. John immediately was out of it. Tony took a few pain relievers to get rid of his headache. His mind wandered that night, but he found much needed peaceful rest.

He was confident in his decision and felt safe even though danger was possibly ahead. His dreams were of the past with his father and grandfather, of everything he'd ever been through, both good and bad, they were a constant reminder of who he had been raised to become, and who he was. John's thoughts were all around the sighting at Mile Marker 9, and the smallest most infinite details of the day. Sometimes he would dream about staring into the wind, as if it was the one thing holding it all together, or the water, almost like it was the thing that held a true constant over time, space, and this great world. Tony's thoughts moved on towards what could be, he could see everything ahead of him, a what if scenario. It's almost like his grandfather was showing him the risks and rewards ahead. He felt himself living the situations out in his head, at night during his dream. It was all so vivid, he didn't feel trapped in some nightmare. Tony felt it was perhaps some spiritual cheat sheet being handed off onto him. He saw a maze, he would turn around every corner and a new surprise would await him. It was all of the pro's and con's he had weighed with his decision to help the aliens, or to destroy them and side completely with the military without question. The military was all he'd ever known in life. It helped him provide a great life and opportunities for his children John and Jenny.

It was even there for him in his great times of loss and sorrow. But, he also knew that it in a way took his father from him, because his father never really acted like a father. His grandfather took on that role with a passion. Tony saw every single thing he had considered. Every plan unfolding, and even a warning of a dark void with a question mark, of something ahead coming to be careful with, but he was not quite sure what it was, or what it meant other than to be careful. Every single piece, all of the positive and negative felt like a giant puzzle piece waiting to be put together, for better or for worse.

Deep in his mind he wondered and wished that his grandfather was there so that he could pick his brain and ask him what to do, but Tony already knew the answer to that question. His grandfather would want him protect life at all costs and to hope above all else, and to show love.

The morning came early. A welcome sound of seagulls could be heard. Mr. Cheverie awoke refreshed and rewards with a confident path ahead. He realized how dangerous it was, but he did not care. He was willing, ready and able to take that chance. All that mattered to him was his family's safety, peace, and protecting the aliens at all costs.

He'd never felt more adamant about anything in his entire life. His normal morning routine was filled out in a timely fashion. He even decided to play along and wear the special jump suit that McGurk had nagged him about wearing. Maybe it would finally shut the guy up. Tony knew, what was on the line. As he zipped the suit up, Chief Cheverie looked into the mirror.

"Chief Cheverie Alien Killer," Tony said.

The patch on the arm actually said 'Alien Killers'. Tony grabbed the fancy aviation glasses McGurk gave him and the files and headed out the door, ready to play the role of a man ready to kill aliens, all while secretly protecting them. Chief Cheverie made his way calmly towards the facility ready to begin. He was not looking back, and he would never give in.

THE TRAINING

Episode 5: Fear the Unknown

The nation is reacting to the fear of the unknown with chaos, while Tony is in his lab trying to understand the alien's biology from a sample of hair he got.

Blacked out helicopters, boats, and vehicles of every kind were descended onto the secret facility. Tony's heart jumped into his throat.

"Are we under attack, by the same peaceful aliens that I chose to trust?" Tony thought to himself.

A man with who had a very advanced looking rifle, pointed his firearm at Tony, ordering him to halt. The Chief revealed his credentials, as well as his access card. He quickly put his palm on the LCD pad which immediately accepted him. The guard stood aside and let him right in.

Chief Reverie walked into the Special Operations facility to a flurry of activity. It was apparent that the feelings of fear and anxiety were the driving forces within the people working so fast that it all seemed like a blur. He had not taken his usual route to the small secret base that day, he had a strange feeling. It's as if someone was telling him to take a path that he hardily takes.

"Could Charlie have been the one who warned me?" Tony thought to himself again. He really had no way of knowing if it was Charlie who warned him, but it's awfully weird that that information popped into his head. Things like that have only happened around Charlie since the Mile Marker 9 incident had occurred.

Tony learned once he arrived at the secret facility that there was another incident. This time a wrecked USO had been witnessed maneuvering through the water and one of the aliens had been catapulted from the USO which was moving through the water very quickly. Multiple witnesses saw the USO make its way out towards the ocean away from land where it disappeared across the horizon, yet it stayed partially submerged underwater.

Tony rushed to the medical ward of the facility, where he saw the alien creature laying on a table. It was breathing slowly. It was dying. He walked up to the alien. It stared back at him intensely. Large black eyes, with very odd and small eye lashes blinked at him, at a pace that seemed in a funky way, human, but it was not human. Its skin was a milky gray color. Even though it was laying on an examination and surgery table, the creature could not have been any taller than about four feet. What laid before Tony and the other men and women in the room looked like the body of a child, but it was an alien.

The Chief quickly put his hazmat suit on as did the other Doctors and Specialists. They were rushing to gather all of their appropriate sensors and tools to take every piece of information about the alien they could gather. Samples of blood, hair, tiny pieces of skin were taken. While this happened, the creature let off these little screams that made Tony's stomach want to turn. It was almost as bad as those miniature electric hand saws used to slice open a person's skull during an autopsy. The table was ice cold. It reeked of death many times over, yet the team was slicing and dicing the creature open. They were only allowed to remove small samples for testing. And ready yet for another mysterious victim to take its last breath, the table allowed a pool of blood to develop. Its blood was along the lines of a blue or green color, not like ours at all. At the hands of covert professionals and specialists, its vital signs which were somehow being measured with electronic sensors, showed that the creature began to fade away. When nobody was looking the alien grabbed Tony's hand squeezing it. He did not know what this meant, other than this creature was as peaceful and loving as what humanity had the capability of being. However, Tony knew that he had to play the role of a wannabe alien killer. As the alien passed away before his eyes he snatched his hand away with disgust, putting on a bit of a show for the other doctors.

"Damn disgusting creature, get away from me," Tony said.

The doctors looked on, as if proud of Tony for rejecting it wholeheartedly, with not even a sign of remorse that it had just died in agony.

Another group of men in black shiny lab suits came into the room with a large black tube. They walked closely beside the tube. One man was looking down at a black and red panel with a screen, while pressing numbers. The tube was meant to transport the now deceased alien body. The crew of medics and specialists watched on as the body was put into the tube, as it was sealed a pressurized steam was exhaled from the tube. A loud beeping sound caused the nervous tension to rise among the doctors. Big white letters were labeled along the side of the tubed container that said, "Wright Patterson Air Base, Underground Level 7." They were so big. It was hard to miss those words. Basically, it meant that Wright Patterson obviously had a secret facility there for either storing, examining or experimenting on the alien creatures. The faces and hands of the men in shiny black lab suits were completely concealed. Nothing on these men was exposed. It was as clandestine as things could get. In all honestly it was quite scary. Tony glanced back at the other Doctors who had already removed their oxygen masks. It's like they were stuck in a trance afraid to move. Chief Cheverie could see the fear in their eyes and sweat on their brows.

"Such a sight it is, to watch grown men tremble, being afraid of the unknown, so afraid it makes them want to go out to their car and get it all over with by emptying a clip into the back of their skull," one man mumbled under his breath to himself.

All of which because they can't explain to themselves rationally what the hell is going on. Hell, it's not like they can even tell their families about the things they have seen at this or any other Top Secret facility. The government would kill them, and their families, or worse, they'd be thought of as insane. And their lives would be ruined forever professionally, privately, and financially worst of all. The group of doctors, other than Chief Cheverie, watched on as the men in shiny black lab suits finished what they were doing with the tube and escorted it out. The entire time, only the one man was typing in a digital command to the black tube. The others just stood alongside it, not even touching it once. And what was really weird, these men in shiny black suits wore very weird metal and plastic helmets and visors. They had no patches or identifying marks on them, where you might see military insignia for rank or what department they would belong to. Absolutely nothing, blacked out, head to toe with weird helmets. Tony noticed that there were no wheels below it, as well. The black tube was floating off the ground, defying gravity by at least three feet. He stared on in complete amazement. A doctor leaned over into Tony's ear.

"Amazing stuff isn't it," the doctor said.

The man faced Tony, man to man, both of which were in their still zipped up lab suits, but their helmets and breathing masks were removed.

Another doctor became noticeably scared, and blurted out loud, "I didn't sign up for this kind of crap. What the hell is going on here?"

Other doctors left the facility to go smoke cigarettes or whatever they could get their hands on to calm themselves down. It was reported an hour later that one of the doctors had committed suicide in the parking lot, because everything that he had seen was just too disturbing for him to handle. Everyone went and got cleaned up, even though there was a protocol to follow. The fact that one of their own had just killed himself because of their secret work, was a bit too much to handle. So, they stopped their work and had meals brought in. Tony sat down with the other doctors as they were all served the meals that they had ordered to be brought in. There were no conversations among them. Just staring at the floor, staring at the ceiling. The only sound that could be deciphered was the buzzing sound of the lights, the many sighs, and boring repeated stirs within cold plates of beef stroganoff noodles.

They knew what was ahead of them, performing tests on what little bit was removed from the alien creatures body. But the question was, who would get the fine privilege of doing such a thing, or things. A man in a white lab coat and slacks walked in, carrying a clipboard. "Jones", was the name on his tag, no first name or last name, just Jones.

"Cheverie," the man called out. Just as his name was being called he was filling his face with a second helping of stroganoff. The other doctors may not have had the stomach to do any eating, but Tony was trying to still play the role of the man with nerves of steel who was ready to kill the aliens. He looked around as his name was called yet again.

"Chief Cheverie," the man said. Tony looked at him almost shocked, but halfway not knowing what to expect.

"Yes?" Tony asked.

The man in the white lab attire handed Tony a clip board. It was white, with black letters. MAJIC eyes only. Chief Cheverie's name was in bold underneath the MAJIC emblem which was in all caps and had a creepy logo of a human and alien hand overlapping. Tony attempted to look through the folder.

The man in the white lab coat put his hand back on the folder, as if to stop him from doing so. Jones looked around the room, and then at Tony saying, "need to know only for you." Jones then walked out of the room saying, "follow me."

It would seem that someone had picked Tony to either be the one to process the small pieces of alien body parts and fluids, or it had been done at random. Perhaps someone was assessing the group's re-action to the one doctor committing suicide in the parking lot. And it was noticed that Tony was the only doctor keeping his cool, with rel-ative ease. Chief Cheverie and the man with the name tag, "Jones", on his right chest, walked down the hallway. Their footsteps echoed, it seemed like miles to go down the corridor. They passed the bath-room on the way to the examination room. Tony could feel his food coming back up, as Jones was walking in front of him. He kept forc-ing it back down. Whoever know playing the role of a stone cold wanna be killer in the military would be so difficult. The end of the hallway had a room which was completely pitch black. Jones walked in first putting his hand against an LCD pad.

"Put your hand on the pad", said Jones.

Tony did as he was told. As his hand was on the panel, Jones swiped his facility card on the side. A green light flickered, and a friendly beep chirped.

"You are now cleared to go anywhere within this facility with your card and with your hand print for use on these pads. From now on when you report to the facility, report to the back entrance. You will be let right in, no more scans at the entrance. Your security clearance has been raised, somebody up top likes the work you are doing, thus they are giving you the chance to try to make a discovery or two for us.", added Jones.

Tony looked at the man in white with a smirk.

"No pressure," added Jones with a simple laugh.

"Yeah, no pressure," grinned Chief Cheverie nervously. When Jones finally left Tony alone to the work, he could not get over the classified technology that was laying on the tables in the room that he would be working with, just to examine the items removed from the alien's body.

Tony walked around the room trying to figure out what to use first. There were scalpels, with electrical appendages big enough to slice a dinosaur open. It made him wonder just what all had been brought to the facility, that's from Earth, which the public knows nothing about. A line to jars were stacked, unused but ready to be filled with the body parts, tissue, or blood of dead aliens. Then again, as Tony looked around in the back of the large laboratory room, he saw filled jars with what looked like unidentified species in the jars, things that the government was choosing to experiment or store away as their chosen dirty little secret. Each jar had file numbers and letters on them, nothing in particular. The names were odd though, nothing that made sense whatsoever.

"Excuse me, Sir, this is not a sightseeing trip," the man in the white lab coat said in a whisper.

Tony thought maybe because it was a man in a white lab coat that it was the same guy who pulled him out of the room while eating. He walked up to the man, and to his surprise even though he sounded like the man who pulled him from the room, it was a different guy, much younger, still even wet behind the ears.

"Sir, they have made you a work station back here, follow me please," added the young lab assistant.

Chief Cheverie followed the young man past a large collection hall of records.

"I thought the laboratory was the room I would be working in. It had a large assortment of advanced instruments," Tony said.

The young man looked at him and said nothing. They came to door. It said, 'temporary exam/ testing room'. The young man opened it. It turned out to be the size of the kitchen where he'd eaten with the other doctors. Quite tiny for a room to perform tests and examinations in. The Chief proceeded into the room.

"Make a list of what you need and it will be fetched for you as soon as possible," added the assistant, whom handed Tony a pen and piece of paper.

Tony scribbled a few things on the list, and quickly handed it back to the assistant.

The assistant laughed, "I don't know if I can get half of this stuff."

The Chief asked for quite a few weird things. A police scanner, a television with all of the news stations, along with a favorite movie channel or two. He requested a high dollar dinner for the other doctors who were not chosen to do the examination, all so they would not feel left out.

A laugh erupted from the lab assistant, "Hahahaha!!! Why do you want these?"

At the very bottom Tony also wanted copies of all of the major newspapers from every major publisher for every day of the week, along with a special assistant to analyze them all for him because he wanted someone to read them for him while he worked.

"You want a special assistant? That we can do for you."

"Not just anyone, its Charlie or nothing," replied Tony.

"Gee Sir, this is above my pay grade. Captain McGurk ain't gonna like this," the lab assistant said.

"Well now McGurk is not here at the moment and I am sure he would not want this operation mucked up by some wet behind the ears freshman from the military academy."

The lab assistant went to work finding everything that Tony had asked for, and then some. Charlie was notified of what he was being asked to do which meant working alongside Chief Cheverie once again, but Charlie already sensed it coming. Within a few hours, the lab assistant had pulled together the impossible list of demands that Cheverie had made including bringing Charlie back in. He was thrilled to work with Tony.

After Charlie walked through the area with all of the fancy tools in order to make his way back towards Tony's new, yet small examination and testing office, he approached Tony with a whisper.

"I think a lot of those tools, were used on humans. I can sense the energy. And I was seeing all types of images in my head. I think that this facility has not just been used on aliens and weird creatures. It's been used to experiment on humans, not just humans in the past either," Charlie said.

"Wait, what are you suggesting?" Tony replied.

"I think they've been replicating the USO's technology somehow. Maybe they have ships close to what the aliens have, and that perhaps they have mimicked some of the alien's behavior and perhaps even abducted people." Charlie's eyes teared up a bit, "They are cruel Mr. Cheverie. I know we promised to help them, but they are very evil and cruel people. When this is over I want out."

Tony held a lone finger to his mouth, "Sh!!!...", in a whisper. "Don't let them hear you say that. Right now you are their golden boy. If you don't help them in some way, there's a chance they may kill you, or worse, Charlotte."

Charlie could feel his heart jump into his throat. The two men got to work. They looked at the blood, as well as other bodily fluids under fine microscopes.

"This is unbelievable," Charlie said.

"What?" Tony replied.

"They are a mixture of aquatic life and plant life. Wait, no this can't be. how can this be?" Charlie added.

Charlie stared intensely into the microscope. He raised his head slowly though just enough to make eye contact with Tony.

"I think they may have partial humanoid DNA within their cell structure. I have seen slides before when I've done stuff for school for extra credit and even for hobbies. I know DNA like the back of my hand. These are without a doubt partial human cells," Charlie added.

"So back up, you are telling me that this thing is part plant, part aquatic life, and it's also part human?" Tony asked.

"Well, yes but it's a very tiny amount of human DNA. I'd even consider it to be junk DNA, but human none the less," Charlie said.

The young man went on to check the skin, hair, hell he looked at everything. Just as Chief Cheverie had and found nothing, but things that were simply beyond his comprehension even with being so educated within the field of biology, he had never seen anything like that before.

Charlie looked at the skin, under the microscope really close.

"Ah cool, these look like fish scales," Charlie said.

All the while they have been compiling a report of any possible weakness that their findings could point to, for anything that could weaken or kill the aliens based on their findings. Charlie and Tony had been working for hours. They decided to take a break. A special portion of the meal ordered for the other doctors was brought to them. They sat down and ate some dinner. It was a steak, baked potato, and a big Caesar salad. Two gigantic orders. They leaned in their chosen seats and watched some television.

Tony was starving so he let Charlie man the remote. He wanted to find a good movie to watch, something with action where the hero gets the girl, but all that Charlie kept finding was anything and everything to do with the news. And wouldn't you guess it, a certain something was being covered time and time again on nearly every Channel. It's as if the country was losing its ever loving mind over the events that happened that day. When Charlie, Mabel, and John went swimming, but got well more than that.

Ever since the Mile Marker 9 incident, the evidence that Mabel, John, and Charlie put on exhibit for the news in their interview has gone viral. Every news outlet across the country has carried their story at least once, some are running it over and over. All of this has infuriated certain parts of the federal government, who has tried to keep these things under wraps for decades. Violent crimes across the country have been trending upwards, as have suicides and murders in general. Polls taken by the media suggest that the existence and proof of extraterrestrial life is beginning to wear on people mentally.

More people are being admitted to mental wards, and being prescribed more antipsychotic medicines to cope. Many people believe that the arrival of the USO's are a sign of the times for the end of the world. While still many people are leading their lives as normal, there are others who walk around with homemade signs protesting. Charlie's face was almost numb from everything he was seeing.

"I had no clue Mr. Cheverie that it was this bad. You do realize this is going to get worse, right?" Charlie asked.

"How so?" Tony asked.

Charlie looked the Chief straight into the eyes.

"Things are escalating quickly. Human behavior can't handle this type of news. Mass suicides will lead way to riots on a grand scale. Not just in the United States but all over the world. Eventually the governments of the world will have to declare martial law within every state, federal and local government. The public will be on edge so much that, they will have lost their collective ability to make rational decisions or even be able to perform objective and logical actions in their everyday lives. We are approaching the end," Charlie added.

"What will stop all of this?" Tony asked.

Charlie laughs. "The only thing I believe will help, is the right thing that you are trying to do, which is garner peace with the aliens. The world has to know that they are here to help us, not hurt us. They are not pure saviors. They have done things they are not proud of on other unruly worlds which they had to get into line, but overall, they are a good peaceful alien species here to help us, to keep us from destroying each other. They realize what a prize our planet is, and they want us to succeed as a race of human beings. They simply hate that we fight each other and are destroying each other," Charlie replied.

"How did you know all of that?" Tony asked.

Charlie sighs.

"I've been having not just visions and remote viewing, but pure psychic experiences. They are talking to me. They are like long conversations now. Sometimes it makes my head and eyes even hurt. Basically, with everything that I now know, and with everything we have discovered here today, we can either bring our two races together at peace and live in harmony or we can destroy them," Charlie replies.

The two men compile two lists. One list on ways to destroy the aliens, but a watered down, dumbed down version a strategic plan for the government to go by. The other is based on all intelligence thus far and from the testing that was just done, to figure a way out how to help and save the aliens, thus the beginning of a plan of how to garner peace between humanity and the aliens.

"I will submit this report. The strategy along with the test findings, everything of which will be dumbed down *etc*. The rest of this will be a blueprint for us to go forward with our plan," Tony adds.

Episode 6: The Set-up

The military is setting up defenses to protect coastal cities and monitoring systems to detect alien Unidentified Submerged Objects.

A group of old men sat around a poker table, drinking ice cold beer and scotch. They had an assortment of snacks spread around like a fat man's paradise. Poker chips, as well as random stacks of ones, tens, twenties, fifties, and hundred-dollar bills, were in loose piles in all areas of the table. Not only were they obviously wealthy, but they were power players in a sense. They were all men who wielded some sort of influence. These men were from all branches of the military some active, others retired. All old, and all of them were well aware of everything involving the alien presence, especially everything going on with the current serious USO situation involving the Mile Marker 9 incident, as well as other similar non-disclosed occurrences. Things that would rock the most normal people to their core, things that were beyond comprehension. Everything from abductions to out of this world sightings that could not easily be explained.

"Thomas, I swear, if you don't stop cheating I will pull my Desert Eagle out and end you right here," John Reynolds, the Secretary of the Navy, threatened with laughter.

One had to ask why a Navy Admiral, the Secretary of the Navy, two retired Army Generals, and a Retired Science Officer, who at one point had his hands in every single classified alien incident the military has worked on, he was known as a brain. Admiral Thomas was making a killing this evening, and at least one of the fellow poker friends that night was beginning to lose his cool. The alcohol was not helping. The other men, their experiences were similar just that, they had experienced things, but not in the position to be smart enough to figure out what to do about it. The room was split as far as how to go about what to do with the aliens. At one point this table of five of the most influential men within the entire United States military took a break from the game. They smoked cigars, and other things that were not legal according to the law.

"Tomorrow is going to be like a day of hell on Earth," Army General Stokes said.

The other General, General Timmons, looked over at him while he chugged his beer. He almost choked on it while laughing. The other men at the table just stared at General Timmons.

"That bad?" Secretary Moss asked.

"You could say that," Timmons said.

"Well, we're all big boys here. Spill the beans. What's under your hat?" the Secretary asked.

"The President has ordered a build up for not just possible tactical assault, but for security measures," Timmons replied.

"Has he been briefed on anything MAJIC?" the Secretary asked.

"No, it's beyond his pay grade, not to mention his security clearance," Timmons replied.

The other men looked at Timmons with old, used up empty looks on their faces. They knew it was true that the President of the United States was just a public face for the people. The leaders of the three letter agencies and the military heads were the real leaders of the country.

"What does he know?" the Secretary asked.

Timmons laughs, "Just what he's seen on the news, just like everyone else. He sees that everyone is losing their minds at this exact moment because of the chaos occurring. He feels almost helpless that he can't keep the public calm. If he knew what we did, it'd probably end mankind as we know it. Let's face it, there are things we've all done, said, and experienced within the MAJIC group that could change the course of history. This USO thing is drawing way too much national attention. This is exactly why we've always kept it all quiet because of something like this happening with the public at large."

"Some of this, if not all, needs to be revealed to mankind. These secrets, they are no good for mankind. People need to know. I mean, our preferred path is peace, but you all are setting us up to get ready for a war that we could not possibly even begin to win," Admiral Thomas said.

The two Army Generals were clinching their respective places at the table. One man, Timmons, had popped open yet another ice-cold beer. His civilian attire was a shirt that looked fit for a golf pro. Timmons' hat was like a sore thumb. It said merely, 'Retired Army General.' The hat was meant as a joke by his grandchildren.

"Say Timmons, when do you think you will actually retire?" Moss asked.

With another big chug of ice cold beer, Timmons responded.

"When we wipe those disgusting aliens from the face of this earth, then I will retire, but before then I will keep fighting the good fight and drinking myself into an open grave all while trying to take down as many of those creatures as I can."

The other Army General, General Stokes, chimed in. "You know, peace would be nice."

He looked around at the other men in the room, "But we all know what's next. It's going to be a war like any other we have ever sunk our teeth into in any of our lifetimes or experiences on the battlefield that we have gone through with fellow human beings."

Stoke stared into his glass of scotch for a moment. He began to tear up a bit.

"My glass is getting too empty," a very drunk Stokes added.

He cleared his throat and brushed away the tears.

"There are no if's ands or buts about it Thomas. We have to kill 'em all. Your boy McGurk is right," Stokes added.

"I honestly do not care what you think. I talked to the other members of the MAJIC group," Thomas said.

The others in the room went silent. The anger was clearly visible on their faces.

"When did this happen?" the Generals asked.

"It was decided to go the peaceful route to keep things from getting worse than what they currently are. I mean have you fellas looked at the news, the newspapers, it's not just the big incident that went viral. There have been similar things happening just like it. People are scared. Some are even killing themselves in massive numbers," Thomas added.

"Good riddance," the Generals laughed out loud obnoxiously as they crashed their alcoholic beverages together in cheers.

"You try to do this militarization crap, and I will stop it with everything I have in my arsenal," Thomas said.

Secretary Moss was quietly sipping his wine and staring at the middle of the table. Essentially Admiral Thomas, and the Retired Science Officer who was also being very quiet, yet drinking and reading, both agreed that peace with the aliens was the answer to carefully handle the situation and not have a martial law type of presence, not just at home in Maine, but throughout the country as well.

The Retired Science Officer was not an idiot, he knew how to stay around. He was a master at longevity within the darker circles of the Federal Government's workings, especially when it came to MAJIC, and other clandestine ventures. He knew that you kept your mouth shut, that you sized up the room, listen to what everyone else had to say, you diagnose the situation. And if they disagree with you, you tell them a bold-faced lie. It's all about survival.

That is how he had survived all these years and been a part of so many alien research and recovery outfits for the government. He knew, that even know there was a right thing to do that he even wanted to do, it could not be done because it would decimate the American public, as well as the world. It was apparent that the General's had other plans in mind.

"So, you are saying, if we put something into motion tomorrow, you will pull your strings and undo what we've been told to do?" Timmons asked.

Thomas looked at the Generals. "Who told you, who ordered you to do that?" Thomas asked.

The Generals looked at each other. "Well, that answer is above your pay grade Thomas," Timmons added with laughter.

Thomas looked at Timmons and Stokes, with a fearful look, as if he'd been betrayed by the group he'd been a part of for decades, MAJIC. Thomas turned to Moss.

"What do you think about all of this?" Thomas asked.

Moss continued to stare into his glass of wine. The man sighed. "We will just have to see how things turn out." Which was not much of an answer.

Secretary Moss was well known for keeping things close to the chest. He was a man of few words. Belches of alcoholic gas that had been stuck up into their nearly retired and not yet retired frames exited from where they came. Some tiny laughter here and there, but the men knew the evening of fun, gambling, drinking and low brow cuts of insane humor was over. The conversation had reached a fever pitch point. You could cut the tension with a butter knife.

The five men went their separate ways. Timmons and Stokes met up about an hour later at a private location. A place where none of the others knew where they would be. As far as they knew from reading the room. Between Mosses reactions and statements, and the RSO who was a very quiet man, they realized their next play.

"I really did not want to do this," Timmons said.

Stokes looked at Timmons with a look that was completely void of sympathy. Stokes lit his cigar. It was the only thing that lit up the night sky around them. Their cars were parked facing each other with the lights off so as to not attract attention. Apparently that was another perk of being high ranking military in such a town, being able to drive drunk or under while intoxicated.

"Thomas is a big mouth. We have to do something," Stokes added.

"Well whatever we do, it can't be traced back to either of us," added Timmons.

"Do you have a Class-C Drop phone with you?" Stokes asked.

"Let me look," Timmons replied.

Timmons walks back to his vehicle, opening the trunk and rummaging through everything. He had guns, grenades, multiple bullet proof vests on hand. There was even a large black case market with the words. "AK-47". It would seem that not only did they carry an arsenal everywhere, but it was apparent that both of these men had a general fear in their lives every single day that they awoke and walked the Earth. They knew that they had enemies, near and far. There was never a moment that they had not looked behind their back waiting for the moment when it was their time to end up in a grave. They knew that eventually they would be expendable even though they were very high-ranking military. Status quo, if you can't be of service, they don't need you anymore. And when they don't need you, you disappear. But worse yet, they do something to you making you live your life eating, drinking, and defecating out of either the same tube or multiple tubes from hospital bed.

Timmons finds a small black box in his trunk.

"Ha, I found it," Timmons with a drunk chuckle said.

Stokes looked at Timmons both shocked and alarmed, "Wait you never activated yours?"

"I never needed it until now," Timmons replied.

"Fine, get the list out. Let's see who we can call to take care of this problem. You and I both know what has to happen within the next twelve hours," Stokes said.

Timmons reached for his glove box. He pulled out a tiny black book of contacts. It's a book that he carries with him everywhere. You never know what situation that you will be in or who you have to call. They thumbed through dozens of pages of hitmen, mobsters, and even killers on parole that they knew of. But they wanted one thing that none of these men and women could even provide, a well-motivated clean kill, all of course something that had meaning. And would put an immediate stop to Admiral Thomas' pending plans to stop the Army General's plans. The flipped through the entire book.

They went past the name that was so obvious. Captain Peter McGurk.

"Wait, why didn't I think of this before? We could get Peter to call the old Admiral up, get hit riled up. We could use some of that old cash that we have stashed. And we could basically pay Peter to find a hitman to have Admiral Thomas killed," Stokes ventured.

Timmons looked at Stokes," Did you just think all of that up? Dammit man, you're a genius."

"How about I call McGurk and you will go get the amount of cash we need. We have what, three million sitting there? I'd say get him out three hundred thousand. That'd be more than enough for him and a hitman," Stokes said.

So from there Timmons left to get the cash, while Stokes called McGurk. The phone rang, and rang. It had to be some thirty attempts, until finally a woman answered.

"Hello?" she asked.

Stokes was silent for a moment, thinking dammit, the last thing we need another eventually loose end. The woman who was drunk and half-asleep laying in bed with McGurk, kicked him.

"Hey, wake up. You have a call Captain," the woman said.

McGurk rolled over and took the phone.

"This is General Stokes. There is an opportunity for advancement. Are you up and willing?" Stokes asked.

"Sir, we are in different branches of the service, but anything that I can do for my country I'm there. What do I need to do? Where do I need to be?"

McGurk wrote the directions down. He confirmed everything with a yes here and there. He then hung the phone up.

"Lisa, I need you to go home. I have somewhere to be," McGurk said.

"But, I'm tired and drunk," Lisa said.

McGurk gave her a hundred dollars cash, "Get out. I have important things to go do."

The woman threw her closes on while cursing under her breath. She called a cab which picked her up.

McGurk knew things were about to get dirty. He'd experienced things like this before. He was alright with that thought. Dirty was his middle name. McGurk went over to his garage and from his row of vehicles he picked out his jet-black mustang. The noise that it made going up and down the highway was rude to say the least.

The meeting place was an old baseball field. It was Timmons, Stokes, and McGurk.

"So, what's all this about at 3 in the morning?" McGurk asked with a big fat smile.

Timmons and Stokes looked at each other and then at McGurk.

"And what's in that fat silver suitcase? Have the powers that be come to me for help?" McGurk asked.

The two men who were overcome with hatred, fear, pride and swelling of negative emotions, were simply filled with ego. Too much ego to admit that McGurk was right. He was being asked for help by them essentially.

"Admiral Thomas has become a problem. He wants peace," Timmons said.

"We want war. Tomorrow there will be the start of a buildup that we have been ordered to begin. However, Thomas has sworn to stand in our way and cause us problems," Stokes added.

"Who wants the build up?" McGurk asked.

The Generals look at each other slowly and then back at McGurk.

"That's above your pay grade. We can't answer that."

The two Generals continued to be silent.

"So, you want Admiral Thomas dead so that you can start this buildup?" McGurk asked.

The men nodded their heads up and down.

"And you want me to hire a hitman and be the third party. Are you paying me as well for this?" McGurk asked.

Timmons proceeded in taking the large silver brief case towards the car's hood. He carefully opened it. McGurk walked over to the case. It was full of fives, tens, twenties, fifties, and hundreds.

"Non-sequential, unmarked, clean, three hundred thousand American dollars," Stokes replied.

"And if you don't follow through, well let's just say that you don't want to double cross us," added Timmons with a very tense look.

McGurk looked grim for a moment, but it did not take long for a big smile to crack the frame of his roughly featured face. McGurk smelled the money. It was an amazing smell to him. He slammed the suitcase closed.

He reached both of his hands out to both of the Generals at the same time with a huge smile.

"Let's go to war, shall we?" McGurk said with the evilest grin anyone on Earth has ever seen.

It even scared the Generals a little. When they went to drive away in their own vehicles, they wondered that even though they wanted to go to war with the aliens. Did they make the right choice? Did they hire the right man for the job?

The clock was stroking close to midnight. An angry old man was having a not so friendly conversation on the phone. Subjects such as morality, judgment, and about how mankind had to show that they were leaders and not full of fear, as far as the alien visitors are concerned. Basically, this was an Admiral chewing out one of his lower level Captains. The General found out the way the aliens were being treated that had come through the secret facility that McGurk was running.

"What kind of operation are you running McGurk?!?!" the old man yelled at him.

Peter, paused, "But, Admiral Thomas, I---"

"I, I, I,... I don't wanna hear it. This is not your Navy, nor is it your military. When you were in diapers I was skull raping the enemy on the battlefield. I don't want to hear your excuses for the actions and behavior of the idiots you have working at the facility or of your own. As far as I am concerned the only man with half a brain there is Chief Tony Cheverie," Admiral Thomas said.

This pissed off McGurk on so many personal and mental levels. He basically could not stand Cheverie, just like Cheverie secretly did not like him either, though the two men remained civil, friendly and acted professional. Maybe it was because Tony was always trying to do the right thing and Peter was always trying to cut, slice and dice corners in any way that he could. McGurk sat and listened to the old man complain more, and he simply just agreed and said, 'yes Sir,' over and over until he was blue in the face. All while this was happening he was texting someone else.

The message read, 'Admiral Thomas, wet work ASAP please, half of $100,000.00 now, half after wet work is complete.'

The person receiving the texts, an unknown hit man, agreed. McGurk developed a calm demeanor on the phone.

"Sir, I understand what you are saying that we can't just jump right in because if we do the public will lose their minds. I understand that we can't just declare open war on these things whatever they are. That we have to go about this in a peaceful manner, that we could learn so much from each other. I agree that we have to be careful and respect the rights of others, and not overstep our bounds," added McGurk.

"Now see. Was it so hard to accept the point of view other than your own McGurk? Keep that attitude up and you might just become an Admiral someday," Admiral Thomas laughed.

Another pause entered the conversation as McGurk suddenly heard Admiral Thomas speaking to another person on the phone, but in the back ground.

"Who the hell are you? How did you get into my house? This is a private residence," the Admiral added in a very worried tone of voice.

The hitman said nothing. A gun however did the talking. A message was being sent loud and clear. The sound of a silencer expelling bullets is heard, though just barely. It was more like sound an arrow makes when it hits its target and the noise seems blunted and quick. Though you could still tell that something was hit by something more powerful. What was more apparent was when the phone hit the floor and with it the sound of a very fat old Admiral crashing down under his now dead weight. The admiral sounded like a three-hundred-pound bag of rotting potatoes falling to the floor without anyone or anything to catch them.

McGurk received a text message, "Wet work done. Pay up," the unknown hitman texted.

McGurk paid the amount owed in full. The next day, it was on the news about the Admiral killing himself at his home. The hitman had made it look like a suicide somehow with note and all. McGurk received a phone call that his command levels were being raised and that he was going to have complete authority to do what was needed to do no matter the cost. Perhaps someone else knew what was going on or perhaps not. Either way, things were about to change quickly and dramatically.

Fog was still rolling off the water as the armed military boats began to make their paths along the waterway. Green and mixed camouflage trucks moved under cover of night along with blacked out vans and SUVS. Planes and Helicopters soared through the air as if doing a grid search or recon. A few Navy ships and submarines were deployed as well. They were ordered to set-up a defensive parameter along all of the coastal cities by McGurk. McGurk had been promised that after getting rid of a certain Admiral that he would be elevated in command, more importantly rank. The Captain would now have the power to decide if the aliens lived or died for sure. They were getting ready for war. He was no longer just a go between guy

with a snarky attitude. With the Captain's orders and the newly discovered information that had been submitted by Chief Cheverie from
the tests that he had completed. Cheverie, who McGurk could not
stand, was actually a valuable asset so he decided to try to make
things work all in the name of killing off the aliens. The military was
going all in with McGurk's orders to not just get into a complete pro-
tective mode, but also to monitor all communications and radar systems on water, under the water with sonar, and in the air if need be.
They said it was to protect, but with the men, vehicles, boats, ships,
etc. deployed. It was war. It had to be.

Episode 7: Undersea Motif

Tony discovers where the aliens are living. His daughter's friend's mother (ELEANOR) leads him to a world under the sea.

The day had begun with excitement. John was ready to go play some football. Even if it was just a practice with his teammates, he loved being able to get out of the house and hang out with his high school buddies. On the way to the practice field John was reacting to things that he was seeing, and not exactly happy with. He was tempted to call his dad, but at the same time, he knew with everything happening that his dad had already been under a ton of pressure and stress, so John let it all just be. He figured that his dad was already aware of what was going on. When John arrived at the practice facility he was the first to show up. With haste he changed into his practice gear. He began practicing his footwork and throwing the football. This was his first time with being back on the gridiron since the Mile Marker 9 incident. He wasn't scared, but he did notice a change within himself. He used to have some attention span issues, now he could focus right in and hit his target. John thought nothing of it. As his teammates rolled in and everyone started running their routes, the others noticed the change in John too. They were happy yet impressed. Their practice ended up being likely the best one they'd ever had as a team. A few hours in, they took a lunch break. John and the other players ventured to the cafeteria where a meal had been prepared for them. John snuck out to call his dad. He was so excited to share the good news. John took the spare cell phone his father gave him and he hit his dad on speed dial. As the phone rang his smile stretched ear to ear. His dad picked up the phone, he'd been laying in bed still trying to wake up from another long night at the lab. Tony had been working a lot after the report work was submitted. Charlie had been a great help with that.

"Hello? This had better be good," Tony said in an annoyed yet sleepy voice.

"Dad, something has happened. When I get home from school practice later this evening I will tell you everything. Just know that you don't have to worry about me anymore," John said with pure excitement.

"What are you talking about John?" his father asked.

Without warning or even cause the phone line went dead. Tony made an attempt to call John back a handful of times with no luck. He became more worried when the line actually came up as "disconnected."

Elsewhere, the opaque shadow of a person watches a rerun of the Mile Marker 9 incident and interview that John, Mabel, and Charlie gave. The person watched the entire documentary and all of the evidence that was presented. When they were done they turned their television off and left wherever they were in a hurry. All faded to black.

Tony laid in bed after he'd hung up the phone. He'd wondered if he had ever moved on and found a girlfriend if she would be making him pancakes or even trying to drag him out of the bed at this precise moment. He shook it off, and turned over in bed. Tony had peace and quiet and he was going to stick to just that. Peace and quiet, though that was the funny thing though. Quiet evenings at home were nice, especially with family or close friends at home to enjoy them with. They come few and far between when John was at football practice nearly every evening and when on the weekends they have double the amount. Tony rested and rested some more. His bones ached. He pondered ordering out for a Pizza. He finally crawled out of bed after he received a text from McGurk's assistant about needing to have extra work done at the lab for a miscellaneous project. Heading out to the Special Operations facility was the last thing that Tony wanted to be doing today. He really wanted to take a day off from everything.

He wanted some adventure added to his day. Even though his existence now included the knowledge of dealing with extraterrestrial life,
at times the mundane tasks involved just seemed so damn boring and
completely annoying. It almost felt as if he was an intern in college
for the Navy, checking and cleaning random specimens, and filing
boring incident reports that he was not supposed to ask questions
about.

Tony had gotten cleaned up and dressed. He even ordered the
pizza he was craving. The delivery boy was there in a flash. He knew
he'd better be if he wanted any sort of cash tip from Tony's wallet.
The kid knew Tony was good for it. As the two made the exchange,
it seemed almost like something out of a spy novel. The pizza kid
looked at Chief Cheverie with worried eyes. The boy sorta poked his
head into the house looking for something.

"Say Mr. Cheverie you guys don't have any aliens at your house,
do you? Because there's a rumor going around that about that," the
pizza boy said.

Tony began to laugh so hard that he nearly lost his stance where
he stood. Mr. Cheverie handed the kid $20 in cash for the $8 pie, in
exchange the kid got a $12 tip. His face lit up with a huge smile.

"Gee Mr. Cheverie you didn't have to do this, but thank you anyways!"

The pizza delivery boy went on his merry way back into town.
He turned back and apologized about the alien rumor question immediately, yelling the whole way.

"Sorry that I asked about that thing. It's a big rumor going
around town."

Tony walked over to the far side of his yard to fetch the newspaper. Another cell phone was in the newspaper. His heart jumped a
few extra beats. It almost sounded like one of those really good 80's
songs that are quite good for dancing to.

"Another one bites the dust," is the exact melody he was thinking of. A stack of paper plates stuck out like a sore thumb in the kitchen, Tony grabbed two and put a few slices on them. He popped open an ice-cold soda while he read his newspaper. The three cellphones sat in front of him. His personal cell phone, the Black Ops cell phone from the newspaper, and the one that McGurk gave him for the Special Operations Facility. One would think that a guy who had been so focused on aliens and doing his government job, but only to the point of helping an alien civilization would be looking for anything in the newspaper that had been happening to help him along. But no, he was not doing so. Tony was admiring the comics section. His favorites were the old lady who had a penchant for sarcasm, Garfield of course. And the zits cartoons, because those in a way reminded him of John when he was a bit younger and before he'd become a bit of a football star. Reading of this quality sorta just helped Tony get his mind off the stresses of everyday life. In a way it made him feel like a kid again, or even like John was little again. Things may have happened back then as well but nothing like they were now.

Tony's face was submerged in the newspaper. A slice of pizza was being chewed and he was reaching for another and a sip of soda. The house was quiet. The only thing that could be heard was Tony's snickering from the tiny little inside jokes in the comics section. It began with a chirping sound. One at a time all three buzzed. You could see this man's eyes emerge from the newspaper as it went down level with the small kitchen table that lay smack dab in the center of it all. Each phone was lighting up, buzzing like well, buzz and vibrate.

To tell each one apart, they had a different color tone. McGurk's was red. It was sort of a joke that Tony felt was appropriate. Tony felt that with McGurk's attitude and demeanor, in the way that he overreacted to absolutely everything thus doing insanely stupid things, that it should be Red. McGurk in a funny way also reminded

Tony in a crazy way of one of the Star Trek television villains, you know the one's with the really funny shaped skulls that have plenty of anger problems, and come off as being really stupid. In Tony's eyes, that was McGurk all summed up. A guy with a fat skull now was a complete and utter dumbass. It's no wonder that most of the people at the Special Operations Facility did not like or even respect the man. Captain or not, he was a jerk. So Tony's choices were not vast. If he did not answer McGurk, then he'd get curious of what he was doing. If he did not answer the Black Op's cell phone he may end up dead in the river within the next few days for no apparent reason. Those people were really easy to piss off. And who knows about the personal cell, the call was a restricted number. Tony answered his personal line anyways. He carefully picked the phone up and placed it close to his ear. All he could hear was static.

"Hello?" Tony asked in a calm manner. At first there was nothing but silence, then a voice fought its way through the crackle. It was Charlie saying, "Mr. Cheverie someone will call you. You have to go." And the rest of what Charlie was saying got lost in the static and his line went dead. Tony trusted Charlie with his life. The kid was almost like a son to him. A nagging feeling kept telling Tony to leave the other two phones at the house, and to just take his personal non-traceable line.

The very moment that he'd decided to give it a go, the personal line rang yet again. This time it was from another restricted number. All Tony could hear was someone who was out of breath.

"Is this some type of sick joke John?" It's not funny. You should be either at practice or heading home for the evening. I've got plenty of pizza left on the table for you to snack on that I just ordered. The heavy breathing continued. And then Tony was quiet.

"Mr. Cheverie, are you alone?" Tony had encountered people using this apparent device that was on the other end before, but it's been a very long time. It sounded familiar but he just could not place it. There was another pause.

"I am, who is this?" Tony asked.

The deep, and odd voice continued, "This is a matter of life and death, yours specifically." Another pause.

"Is that a threat, are you threatening me?!?!" Tony replied with outrage. He began to get pissed off. "Do you know who I am. I am a Chief with the United States Coast Guard," Tony replied in an aggressive manner. "And just who in the hell are you?" Tony asked further.

The breathing slowed, and with a sigh. Tony heard this, "We know who you are Mr. Cheverie. If you want to live, you will meet with us immediately."

Tony is texted coordinates. He lined them up on a map, and they are for one county to the west of where he currently was, near the big lake that Charlie, Mabel, and John have gone swimming for years. It just happened to be the same lake they were on their way to the day of the Mile Marker 9 incident. The voice went on to tell him to drive carefully, that eyes were everywhere. At first, he wondered if he should perhaps use his truck to go check out the lake and meet whomever the wacko who just called him was. Tony walked out to his garage, where a Harley Davidson, which was covered by a huge black tarp was parked. The Chief removed the dust, which was very little because of the cover. He smiled and said to himself, "Have not ridden you in quite some time my beautiful."

He reached over towards the spare can of gasoline. It was filled with just enough fuel to fill the tank up. Tony wiped the speedometer off. "The last thing I need is to get pulled over for speeding," he said laughing to himself.

Chief Cheverie sped off, with the sun on his back and the wind in his face. He'd adorned a shiny black biker's helmet, black leather jacket and blue jeans. It was honestly the best idea going into something like this, to go dressed as a civilian for something that's so off the books, especially when he did not know exactly what to expect. It was such a random event, getting called by that type of voice on his personal cell phone. For his Black Ops phone that self-destructs which he gets from the newspapers at times, that was understandable. This was just weird all around. The ride was a bit boring but still he had not done anything like this in quite a long time. Tony wanted an adventure to get out of the house. He was getting one. Closer and closer the wheels on the bike grinded, bringing him to the lake a foot and a mile less farther away. He'd see the signs for the lake with so many miles away from 10, to 9, to 8 and so forth, until about fifteen minutes later he reached the exit for the lake. Nervous sensations were pulsating through him again. He began to second guess himself for not bringing the other two cell phones, but at the same time he thought, 'well they could track me with those, so it's a good thing that I actually did not bring those along for the ride.' A smell of water and the sound of fish biting sounded and smelled so inviting to Tony's senses. He knew that he had arrived. Splashing sounds were practically calling his name in a playful manner, yet Tony knew he had other business to tend to there. But what? Who had called him in such a crazed manner? Who was it that apparently knew him so well? He pulled his personal cell phone out, and turned it on, both hoping and dreading for the mysterious caller to call back yet again. And to either his surprise or complete dread once more, the restricted caller, came calling. The heavy breathing and the pause.

"Mr. Cheverie, are you here?" Tony looked around alarmed. He saw no one.

"Look, I'm through playing games. You either come and meet me right where I am right now or whatever this is done, it's finished," Tony added.

The deep voice chimed in, "Look we can't meet you in the open. It is not safe for you, or for us."

The Chief began to wonder if there was perhaps another person within the Facilities operations that was turning whistle blower on everything that had been going on. Those types of things never end well for the whistle blowers or for the other people involved with the eventual whistle blowing. The government is not to kind and open about such things. It's sorta true what you see in the movies. When they disavow you, they really mean it. When you turn your back on them, they turn their back on you and then some. Meaning, they contact someone to help make you disappear if possible.

The dark voice pauses, and then coughs. "Walk away from the Harley, Mr. Cheverie," the voice added.

"So they can see me. I just wonder what part of this area that they are really in?" Tony pondered. Keys were in the ignition. Tony pulled them out, not wanting anyone to steal his pride and joy, even though absolutely nobody was around. Which was sorta odd for that town on a nice day like it was. Normally on a day like this, tourists would have this place packed. Boats would be sliding down the delivery ramp to go fishing on the lake. Kids with their families would be picnicking over near the covered pavilion. And there would probably even be some tiny little social event or fair even going on that was family and pet friendly Their town was the type of small coastal town to put things like that on. The mayor was the type who was always trying to think little things up to draw people to their little corner of heaven. In a way, with everything that's been happening it's been feeling like a secret clandestine corner more than anything here lately.

Tony had the cell phone held out and on speaker phone so that he could hear this person, or persons commands loud and clear. He began to walk away from the motorbike. Even though he had the keys, he still feared doing so.

"You are getting warmer," said the dark deep voice in a playful manner.

His steps picked up, getting closer to the water, until finally he was at the edge of where the landing ramp meets the water itself. The dark deep voice, which sounded yet strangely familiar and odd paused.

"Why did you stop?" the voice asked.

"You told me I was getting warm," Tony said.

A commotion was heard as if two people were giggling and fighting over a cell phone or similar electronic device. He listened for a moment.

"Hey who is this? Is this some kind of sick joke to fulfill your weekend?" Tony asked.

Everything went silent. And then a pause with deep breathing.

"Step closer, you are on fire," added the voice.

"If I step any closer, I'll get drenched," Tony said.

The voice sounded impatient this time.

"That's the point. Down here with us, you will have to get wet eventually." Another pause, along with commotion and laughter. Tony was getting, both angry, annoyed and well he was still sort of scared. He wondered just who the hell it could be, and what their aim was. The voice continued, "Walk out just a little more."

"OK, the water is now up to my ankles. It's getting real. What is this?! Some type of joke?! What am I looking for? Where are you?" Tony asked.

"Be patient this is not an instant thing. He we are," added the voice.

Tony saw something odd poking out on the top of the water. It was the very top of a mini-submarine. It had to be about twenty or thirty feet long, big enough for maybe five or six people. He knew because of the model number. For years he had to study submarines as part of a Coast Guard course to figure out the best route to go about studying undersea life. He had to help hand pick and partially design a few.

The submarine did not lift from the water completely. Just enough for the hatch to open.

"Mr. Cheverie, hop in, and close that hatch behind you," the voice said.

He thought to himself, "I'm either going to die now and nobody will ever see me again, or I am about to discover something amazing."

Tony who got even more wet this time as he climbed deeper into the water but had to pull himself up on the side of the partially still submerged sub to actually get to the open hatch. He stood at the top of the ladder in the sub, slowly making his way down, and he pulled the hatch down behind him, rolling the wheel until he heard a tight bolt locking and compressing the entire sub safely shut. Dripping water all around him, the normal sound of a sub, along with the distant echo of a running engine, these things matched his somewhat fear filled heartbeat. The light that captured his eyes was a bit more welcoming. He turned around the corner of the tiny vessel and he was met by a person running at him from a shadow. He was scared because he had no weapon to defend himself, so Tony just stood there and would take the brunt force of whatever came his way. And out into the lone emergency light of the sub ran his daughter Jenny, hugging him tightly.

"Oh my god," she cried, "you're safe."

Tony embraced her. He had not seen her in quite a while.

"I saw Johnny on the news with his friends. I knew that if I showed up and told you about everything that they would follow you," Jenny added.

"Wait, you knew who would follow me?" Tony asked.

"Dad I've known for as long as you've been in the Navy that you've been involved off and on in "odd", yet borderline clandestine stuff. I used to wake up to you and mom arguing and her going out drinking, and then you on the house phone talking about seeing certain top-secret things," Jenny said. His daughter looked at him like a consummate pro, "I know everything."

"So I figured I'd lure you out here safely," his daughter said.

"But why?" Tony asked.

A girl walked around the corner from the shadows. "Dad this is my friend Eleanor. We found something you might want to see," his daughter added.

Eleanor and Jenny guided Tony over to a workstation bridge area where an older man, Eleanor's uncle, was commandeering. Her uncle waved at Tony with a friendly smile and a 'hello.'

They began to glide into the lake, going deeper and deeper. Eleanor had something in her hand, and she clicked it.

"Mr. Cheverie, pay attention," she said with a laugh. It was the small electronic object used to make the deep odd sounding voice on the phone when they called him.

"Kids," Tony laughed and scoffed. The four of them sat in Captain's Chairs buckled in as they saw them coming into focus. Green lights, many of them. There were also oval shapes, disc shapes. Some of them were flat, some were perfect circles, others even cigar shaped.

"What is this? What am I looking at?" Tony asked.

Her Uncle looked over at Tony, simply saying, "I may be a rich man, but I have a weird hobby of going underwater and screwing around in my submarine. I found this, and I told Eleanor, who in turn, shared it with Jenny."

The girls added in at the same time, "We felt you needed to know. You'd know what to do."

Tony was still trying to take it all in. There had to be at least two dozen USOs down there and what looked like an alien base. It was an

alien base, he was rubbing his eyes to make sure they were not playing tricks on him. Not just green lights, but subtle red and purple
would phase in and out.

"This is nothing," Eleanor's uncle added.

The four of them in the sub took a different passage underwater.
"That's just a small piece of this pie," her Uncle added.

The submarine ventured towards an area that fed out to the Atlantic Ocean.

"You see, under the lake, there's a waterway that they built into,
and as you can see ...", her Uncle added.

He pointed out to the Atlantic Ocean seafloor. There was a massive Alien underwater settlement and base. It had to five times the
size of an American Football Field. Tony was in shock.

"There are four more just like this. Yes, I ventured out there and
saw them. Each one is a bit different. Hundreds if not thousands of
USOs," her uncle added.

Her uncle handed Tony a DVD with all of the footage he recorded. Tony was in shock and awe struck. What they just gave him
was blowing this entire thing wide open. He'd have to play dumb.
The military would eventually find all of this. Tony returned home,
while Jenny went to her friend's house for the night to hang out. He
walked in and was a bit alarmed. John was nowhere to be found. The
sun was going down, and the pizza he had ordered, which was John's
favorite, had not even been eaten other than what Tony ate before he
left. He called his son's cell phone, no answer. Tony headed straight
for the school. Scared as hell fearing the worst.

THE BATTLE

Episode 8: Phase One

Armed military monitor everything, work places, the grocery stores, hospitals and especially coastal towns.

It went off like an alarm in Charlie's head, the urge to call Tony and to trust the person with the deep voice, to go meet them, that no harm would come to him. But when Charlie tried to call, he could barely hear Tony. It's almost like there was some sort of satellite or static interference. After Charlie hung up on Tony, he had that weird feeling again, that nagging sensation. Something told him to write the book. He pulled out all of his notes. Every single picture, every folder, even his personal copy of the interrogation. Along with his copy of the DVD that Tony gave him. All while Tony went off to meet whomever, Charlie had been assembling everything to write his book. Not just for the Mile Marker 9 incident, but his book of strange occurrences he'd endured within his entire life. In about a four-hour span, he'd typed 20,000 words. He was like a machine.

He had an urge. It was like an itch that he could not scratch. The only thing was, he could scratch this itch. And it was all about an interview. A certain particular person to be exact. With his hand almost seeming possessed, he dialed McGurk's number. He left a message asking for the Captain to call him back, that it was very important, that he had to ask him a very important question. And for good measure to make things dramatic, Charlie asked McGurk to call him back as soon as possible. It wasn't even five minutes and Captain McGurk, called Charlie right back.

"Hello? Charlie, lad how are you?" McGurk asked.

"Great Sir. I don't know if you would mind or be interested, but I'd really like to interview you for a book that I am writing about the military. Charlie told a lie. It happened to be a big damn lie. He intended to write something upon the subject of the clandestine activities going on and aliens, involving everyone. Charlie's ultimate intent was to expose them all. However, he decided his chances for information and alternative points would be better if he fibbed and told

87

them the subject matter was different. McGurk agreed, and Charlie made his way down to Special Operations Facility. McGurk was not in his normal office. He was in a conference room that was possibly ten or twenty floors below ground. He said he had a meeting and that he was waiting for the rest of the parties to get there.

Before leaving his house, Charlie locked away all of his copies of his evidence in a place that only he knew of for safe keeping. Charlie caught a cab from his house. He carried just a tape recorder and a black ink pen with a note pad. He also carried his backpack, with other odds and ends, along with a camera. When he arrived at the facility not many people were that it was like the place was deserted or almost shut down. Some people were moping around, as if the end of the world were near. Others were cheerful and ready as if a party we're about to go off at any second.

That funny feeling hit him again. Uncomfortable flashes came into his mind. One of his full episodic blackouts where he sees things like the future or what might be going on in another place, just happened to be taking place. He stood there like a statue. Nobody bothered him. The young brainy fellow was known quite well at the facility now. Henceforth, nobody questioned his coming and going, nor did he rarely get asked about his Facility identification unless it was a new security guard on duty for a shift. He froze dead in his tracks. His breathing became limited as if someone was standing on his chest.

He thought, "I'm too young to have a heart attack, I'm in love with Charlotte and way too good looking to die young."

As Charlie straightened his glasses out, he focused. It was like a moment in time that was frozen. Everything had stopped around him. But at the same time, for a sheer moment in time, everything around him was gone. And his sight delivered only one mind refining transformation, thanks to his wonderfully sensitive gift. The visions he saw were opaque, yet they were like scenes from an old movie. The color was there, though subtle. He saw a young man with glasses who reminded him of himself. The young man was being followed. He kept seeing blood flowing on a floor, and even hearing a loud bang. There was a glimpse of a few random men with those particular department store hats' which look like the belong on the head of a vacuum cleaner salesman. They even wore the same thing that the average detective at a police department would wear. Charlie only knew this because Charlotte's father was a detective with the local police department, and he dressed essentially like a business man.

The horrible vision trampled through Charlie's mind over and over. What seemed like hours, or days, went by in the motion in a minute or two. He stood there with his controlled breathing and deciphered the message as it came to him in completion, even though it was one of dire circumstances which involved him. His strong psychic instincts were telling him that McGurk would eventually try to have him killed. The timeline for such a thing would be sped up however because of the interview that was about to take place. Though he had another feeling a small shred of hope about something. On one hand, he's getting a message about who is going to kill him, and that he's going to die. And on another hand, he's receiving some strange message of hope. All he knew to do was to go forward with the interview, even though he was just a touch nervous. Charlie walked into the building after pressing his hand on the LCD screen that required his hand print. When his vision ended everything instantly unfroze as if time had been restarted upon Charlie's individual account. At times, he still had to get used to it. His own day-to-day life was feeling like a supernatural / science fiction book other than the crazy things he was now involved in with at the Special Operations Facility. The young brainy one walked into the facility and people were so happy to see him. Word had gotten around about Charlie's abilities to see things. Three women who worked in the facility doing payroll, but on a non-disclosure basis stopped to ask Charlie questions about their families and one about a loved one who passed on. Before they could say a word, he already knew their questions.

"Darla, no your husband is not cheating on you. He's actually working late to save up for that cruise you've been begging him about. Shelly, if you add this particular list of food to your diet regimen, you will lose weight."

Charlie wrote down a list of things and quickly handed it to the woman.

"Oh, and Delores, the answer is yes," Charlie said. He didn't say what 'yes' was to, but she smiled anyways. All of the women were so much happier for knowing the little that he had just shared with them.

"It's truly amazing how one small detail can change a person's life overnight," Charlie thought.

Charlie stepped into the elevator when he remembered how many floors down he had to go to meet McGurk.

"Twenty floors down, sheesh, hope I don't end up getting sick from the ride," Charlie moaned.

The elevator kept stopping and starting. People kept getting off and on from other floors. It became an elevator game of musical chairs. Some thirty minutes later, the janitor got on at the third floor. Both Charlie and this old man rode down to the twentieth floor. At the moment the door opened, there was a long dark hall which had lights at the very end.

The very old janitor simply said, "Last stop, unless your next destination is hell."

Such an eerie fellow the janitor was. Charlie creeped out of the elevator slowly as he watched the older man shuffle off down the hall. He watched the janitor push his yellow bucket with mops into a closet.

"That's odd," Charlie thought. "Why have a broom and mop closet this far below the surface?"

The young man stood there as the older man walked back towards the elevator and he watched as it crept back up to the surface. The hallway was Empty. It was void of sounds. Yet, there were other doorways that were blacked out. On these doors, there were many languages that Charlie could not understand. However, with his not so subtle gift, he began to see anyone and everyone involved with each room. Things came to mind concerning off the book projects, things concerning planetary security and other alien species. The walk was some twenty yards in length. When Charlie came to the door, the lights were bright. A long table laid ahead through might double doors. On the side was a mini eat-in kitchen with food as well as drink machines. Charlie's stomach rumbled like a pitiful dog.

"Should've eaten before leaving," Charlie thought.

When he opened the doors to the big conference room, the air hit him and it felt oh so comfortable. It was like a rush of cool air compared to the stagnant air of the rest of the facility for the most part. Charlie was just thankful he did not have major breathing allergies.

Charlie pulled his bag off his shoulder and sat everything down on the table. He got ready, placing the tape recorder next to his notepad which had the fake book title written on it. "My Military Pride". His stomach rumbled yet again. Charlie knew he would not get much done on an empty stomach, and it would probably mess with his concentration. He looked inside his wallet and pockets. There was no money. However, something from the seat next to him caught his eye. It was shiny. A small bag of coins someone had left in the seat. It was tucked away. Charlie pulled the small bag close to himself, finding many dollars' worth of change. He pulled five dollars out to eat off of. He was starving. Even though his stomach was begging, he figured whomever left the money would understand his plight. When Charlie pulled the small bag of change in his direction, he accidently pulled the chair his way as well. He did not notice all of this until after he had already paid for all of his food. Now Charlie had a pile of delicious junk food sitting on the conference table.

The item that was on the floor under the chair was a wallet. It was filled with hundreds of dollars. All of them made the wallet to the point of barely being able to close. Again, he felt bad about someone losing their money. He didn't even look inside to see who it belonged to. He just tucked it into his pocket. Somebody would ask about a missing wallet eventually. Without warning the big double doors pushed open just as Charlie had shoved the wallet into his pocket and put the bag of change away.

In walked McGurk, and with him he brought both the smell of the stagnant facility and that feeling, the rush of death. As if everything had already been planned. Charlie could see it in the man's eyes. He intended to have him killed quite soon. Charlie felt hopeless, though that one small little voice said, 'hang on, hold on, help is on the way, don't give in, don't give up.' There was still a good feeling in the back of his mind, outweighing all of the bad. McGurk pulled a chair out and got as close to the table as possible.

"So now, Charlie, what do you want to ask me?" McGurk asked.

At that exact moment McGurk seemed cheerful and excited. Charlie thought, 'well I guess he's already planned my murder that's why he's so damn happy, or perhaps Chief Cheverie's.'

Charlie begin ringing questions off, one at a time. He threw a few the Captain's way to get him comfortable and even to make him laugh. And then though questions came, the ones meant to put him on the spot.

"Captain, please explain your stance on the current alien war situation that the military is involved with and dealing with," Charlie said. McGurk was stunned.

Speaking cleanly and carefully into the tape recorder, McGurk said, "Well, the current situation is one of a sensitive nature." Then McGurk asked, "Is this on or off the record?"

Charlie responded, "It's off the record, but on whenever."

Charlie was smart. He knew when to say what to confuse McGurk. The idiotic Captain thought nothing of it. He began to answer the question more thoroughly, practically giving up every nugget of information that Charlie had been actually seeking for his book. He tossed another question McGurk's way, this time it was about the interrogation.

"Captain, can you please tell me what you thought of the alien interrogation in room 5?" Charlie asked.

Again, the Captain looked alarmed and perplexed. He almost forgot that Charlie was sensitive. McGurk was not the sharpest tool in the shed, just an angry tool. That was the best way to describe that man. The interview questions continued, getting tougher and putting the Captain on the edge even more, to the point he was looking at his watch wondering when it all would be over.

Finally, Charlie asked McGurk, "Is there anything this war has made you do that you regret doing, or that you plan on doing?"

The Captain had an empty look on his face.

"No, I've had to do things, many things to get things done. All of which were a questionable nature, but they were in the name of National Security. I regret nothing," McGurk said angrily in a loud voice as he pounded his fist on the table.

Charlie already knew that McGurk had Admiral Thomas killed and he knew he was next. The double doors burst open. People began to flow in for the meeting. Charlie quickly packed up everything and stopping the tape recorder and gathering all his notes.

"Thank you so much for the interview Captain McGurk, this book will rock thanks to you," Charlie said.

The young man caught McGurk off guard and grabbed his hand and quickly shook it, leaving the Captain dumbfounded. One of the people who walked in was the Secretary of the Navy, Mr. Moss. The man was looking around a chair.

"Anybody see a bag of change and a wallet, mine fell out. When I went to lunch and I had to put it on my tab."

Mr. Moss looked around and nobody seemed to be helpful. Charlie knew this was his chance to do the right thing.

"Sir, I found it." Charlie pulled the stuffed wallet from his pocket along with the change bag.

"I hope it's alright that I took five bucks out, I was starving," Charlie added.

Mr. Moss walked up to Charlie. He put his hand out and shook his hand in a jolly manner, quite the opposite that he was dealing with from Captain McGurk.

"Anything else you need Charlie?" asked Moss. Charlie smiled and shook his head.

"No thank you Sir, but thanks anyways."

Charlie walked out and quickly rode the elevator up the stairs. He wanted to leave the facility as soon as possible, especially with all of the juicy questions he got McGurk to answer candidly. And best of all, Charlie felt like he had just made a new friend with Mr. Moss. He honestly had no idea how much of a friend, he'd made. The meeting began and the fine points of the intelligence gathering were gone over. McGurk had his report that he was given by Tony.

"You know, Captain, that young kid Charlie sure is something. We could use more honesty like that in this room, in the ranks, don't you think?" Moss asked.

McGurk, grinded his teeth. The red veins in his eyes begin to poke out and find alternative pathways to hammer home the utter tension that was erupting within his cranium.

"Yes, Sir. Great kid," McGurk added.

Before the Captain could say another world, Moss was looking over the report handed in by Tony.

"And this Cheverie fella, what a great guy, top of his class. Always there and reliable, nothing to doubt about him. That right there is a soldier," Moss added.

McGurks face was so red you'd swear someone just plugged a fire department hose into it to put a fire out. He was pissed off, sick and tired about hearing all the good things about Tony Cheverie and especially Charlie. He once thought well of both of them but he felt as if they did not have his best interests at heart anymore. Especially with the questions that Charlie had the gall of asking him. Moss spoke over the sudden commotion in the room.

"In three hours, I want us everywhere. I want an armed presence monitoring any and every place possible all across the country, and especially the coastal cities. Monitor all communications. Everything from the workplaces, to the grocery stores. Don't forget the hospitals, and especially the coastal towns. All intelligence is important. These are orders from the top. This new war against these alien races, it's something far past any of our past experiences. We are casting a massive dragnet for intel over not just this state but all states to find anything relevant and use it. The most important areas are bodies of water and areas where sightings of USO's have been reported near said bodies of water."

What Moss was not telling everyone else, was that there was a mole within the group who was also selling secrets to a foreign government or hacker group for high dollar. Every member of that committee, as well as all members of the facility, would have a new CIA handler following them, as well as an NSA analyst combing over all data created by each person, to weed out questionable activity and to find this mole. Moss was told so by the head of the CIA, that someone was not only helping the enemy but selling secrets. It was a need-to-know-basis sort of thing. From there the meeting was adjourned. The Captain jumped on the elevator relieved that he could actually have a second alone to breathe. He closed his eyes as the elevator doors closed. He was expecting a peaceful ride to the surface. That was not to be so. When he opened his eyes, the slim frame of Mr. Moss had snuck onto the elevator just before the doors closed.

"Got it!" Moss, who was a bit short on breath, added.

The two made small talk that was not much. Their eyes were concentrated on the lights on the elevator as they chimed with every number counting. 20...19.... 18... 17... McGurk's heart began to jump quicker. He could not wait to get out of the building, hell, out of the elevator would be nice. The elevator suddenly stopped and the lights went out, an odd sound noting an alarm turned on the emergency lights. At first there was subtle panic between the men.

"Nope, we need to keep calm. We are still fifteen floors below ground level. We only have so much oxygen. We need to keep calm and conserve it," Moss said.

The men sat in silence for about thirty minutes. "Say, did you hear about what happened to old Admiral Thomas?" Moss asked.

"Yeah, that's really sad. I thought he was a great man. It's sad that someone would shoot him like that," McGurk replied.

There was a pause and then Moss responded.

"There is an investigation that's being opened into it. It's being called a possible murder. There are signs of foul play."

"Oh?" quipped McGurk with sudden panic.

His eyes went empty again, but he responded to Moss, more to attempt to cover his own ass, "Yea I can still remember that old dog from back in the day. He was tough but he kicked us all and kept us all going."

Moss replied, "Yeah he did. It's too bad some asshole had to go and do this. We're gonna throw the book at them. I was told they are seeking the death penalty and everything once it's found out who did it, or well at least who had a hand in doing it."

McGurk again looked panicked and sweated up a storm. He had no clue that Moss might think that he was the one who killed Thomas. It was also true that Moss, could not stand McGurk either. Moss knew that McGurk was a bit off, and was capable of doing things that bordered upon the lines of insanity.

"So, there's an investigation?" McGurk asked. He shook his head, "That's just great. They need to find the killer and give it to 'em good," McGurk added.

Moss smiled at him, somehow amused.

"Yep."

The darkness and quiet began to make McGurk's mind wander. His eyes closed and then opened again. He breathed slowly and get his metal briefcase. He stood up and over Moss, who looked up at him to ask what the hell he was doing? McGurk took his suitcase and began to beat the hell out of Moss, soaking the elevator with his blood. When Moss could not fight back, McGurk began slamming his head into the elevator doors. The blood more so began to splatter with fury. McGurk screamed out loud. He awoke with Moss shining a small light in his eye.

Moss whispered, "You passed out. I think it's because of oxygen deprivation."

McGurk agreed, and told Moss, "to shut up and save the oxygen."

The two rode the uncomfortable ride of silence to the top of the elevator. They left and went their ways. McGurk was on the phone with his buddy who did the Thomas hit. He was asking for another favor, that he had another loose end to take care of, perhaps two. And then Moss was on the phone with his friend at the CIA and the other at the NSA, asking that the discussed protocol be initiated immediately, to have the list of people followed and have all forms of communication tapped, all data farmed and checked. From there Moss headed to Washington, D.C. to meet with the Joint Chiefs of Staff to put into motion all of the paperwork to start the communications build up to monitor everything. They were ready, willing and able to protect and destroy whatever was to come their way, now they just had to listen. Their goal was to find the mole and to find those who were meaning to work against them by any means necessary.

Episode 9: Secret Agent

A secret agent finds out where the aliens are living, and the plans for battle began. They also find out that Tony is associated with them.

A briefing rolls across the desk of an Agent's desk. It's a special request from Captain McGurk's himself. The man reads it and his face tenses up. He nearly loses his lunch in one breath. Fear rushes through his extremities with violent excitement.

"Could it be?!" the man thought.

The man in question is an agent for the CIA, Agent Roman. He'd been told to follow Chief Tony Cheverie after the Mile Marker 9 incident to be certain of where his true loyalties were. Agent Roman wondered if Chief Cheverie was some spy against either his own government or against the human race. As soon as news of the incident hit the intelligence wire, not even Moss knew about what McGurk was asking of the CIA Agent. There were even undercover CIA following Captain Peter McGurk around and he didn't even know it at the request of other parties, though Agent Roman has no knowledge of this. Clever, yet sneaky they are, they lurk in the shadows like a bad taste in your mouth. They are careful, yet they know how to hide in plain sight if they need to. The Agent had been tracking Tony's movements for quite some time. He followed him to the park for the meeting with the Black Ops Agent at three in the morning. And he followed him to the lake, after he intercepted the call Tony received from the 'anonymous' caller with the deep voice. The Agent followed Tony until he reached a point on the highway in which he could hide. From there, the Agent deployed a new version top secret drone which ran in a stealth manner. Sunlight bounced off of it, and it did not give a heat signature nor did it create any sound. It was merely a device to track and collection information on subjects of all kinds. Roman sat in his concealed, blacked out SUV as he watched the drone footage of everything Tony was doing. He could not believe what was happening.

"Come on, who are ya meeting?" Roman said to himself rhetorically.

He watched Tony walk closer to the water. The Agent nearly spilled his hot coffee in his lap when the object emerged from the lake slowly. It was a submarine.

"Bingo, wait, what? Who are these people? Humans?" Roman said, scratching his head in confusion.

His mission to watch Chief Tony took a turn for the boring as he realized the so called hot tip from the top to watch certain people turned out to be nothing more than a misfire of power. The Agent eventually dozed off through the entire drone's operation. The drone could also venture underwater. It was waterproof and it could not be detected by sonar or any motion detectors. Its technology had not been made available to the public as of yet. Before dozing off, Roman watched the footage as Tony got into the submarine and it submerged. He felt it was becoming the wild goose chase of a Jacque Cousteau wannabe. From there he lost his ability to give a damn about the entire mission. He'd been away for twenty-four hours. He turned his phone off and had hit screw it. The drone was on an artificial intelligence timer mode. When it was hitting 'sensitive' territory, it would alert its handler, who just happened to be Agent Roman. When the Agent woke up, the drone was returning. And a multitude of red alert sensitive beeps came across his laptop screen in the SUV. They were pictures and footage of everything that had occurred underwater. Showing everything from where Tony and the submarine had gone, to what all had been seen, including the underwater alien bases, the USOs, and visible alien life living underwater. Roman was in shock. He'd seen some things in his time with the Agency, but this type of footage would land him either a job with a higher pay grade along with clearance or it would find him in a watery grave if he handed it to the wrong people. He decided to tread carefully.

The footage showed Tony leaving the submarine and heading back towards the Agent's direction which happened to be parked on a highway and concealed. The Agent pushed a button and the color of the SUV changed to a dark blue. And another button changed the shape of the body frame ever so slightly to make the vehicle appear thus more different. And thus the same thing was done again to show the vehicle was not government, but an out of state tourist. The Agency was always thinking ahead of itself. The best way to watch people was to pretend like you it belonged there as well. Roman waited for Tony to drive along. He kept waiting, but nothing. The only thing he did get that explained why everything took so long, was some grainy footage that was delivered from his drone that showed a bright light coming up against Tony while he was driving the motorbike. And then the drones screen went to white, then to static. It flashed and Tony had disappeared. Elsewhere other eyes which were not human we're also watching all of this happen. They had taken note and reacted with what they felt was something appropriate. The drone waited in that precise location from a safe distance some twenty minutes later, and Tony reappeared on his motor bike going on the same exact direction at the same exact speed with the same white flash on the screen and glimmer of static. Roman looked at the time stamp which showed it to be exactly twenty minutes from when Tony disappeared. He just captured something amazing in his drone footage. Within moments, Tony drove his motorbike by the Agent's location. Slowly the Agent pulled out of hiding spot. He kept a careful distance. While driving, the invisible drone landed on his SUV. Roman followed Tony to as he made his way to the school.

The motorcycle almost did not want to go as quickly as Tony wanted it to go. Anticipation and fear ran through Tony's body as if he was on fire. He was on edge. He feared the worst.

"John never goes without answering his phone or at least getting back with a response as soon as possible," his father thought.

The wind whipped steadily into Tony's face, as he had the visor up on his helmet. Sweat percolated all over his body. It was nerves. Being threatened by government creeps in trench coats at three am seemed to make Tony's blood run ice cold. He could handle that as if it was second nature. He was so damn used to it, such things had in a way been happening off and on for years, even though things have ramped up because of the events recently. The Chief's focus beamed directly onto the winding highway like a laser ready to strike at any moment. His heart pumped so fast he thought it might run up his throat and outpace the motorbike. Tony looked at the speedometer. It said 80 mph, but it felt as if it was going so much slower, as if reality itself kept holding him back. A trip that would normally would take five to ten minutes tops, seemed to be approaching the half hour range. More time slipped by and Tony noticed this same occurrence. Another five- to ten-minute interval along another winding highway. There were only so many winding highways in that area. He became more alarmed. He wondered if somehow, he had just experienced a form for "time loss" during his ride to the High School. He had no memory of stopping anywhere else, or of anything odd happening to him. All he had to go on was the fact that he noticed his trip took longer than normal. He had about twenty minutes that he could not account for. Something was off. Something was most certainly not right.

The school was set a few blocks away from the ocean itself. The football field was positioned in a way so that the wind coming off of the beach would somehow give the home football team a slight advantage. It really only helped whichever team had the wind at their backs during a game. It helped the ball fly farther. In a way, it gave a boost to the running backs. And some would say it did add a good five yards onto those very long field goal attempts their team was known for making. The very moment that Tony's motorbike reached the school, the sun had already gone down. He had flipped his headlight on not long ago, so driving into the parking lot, it would not exactly be easy to identify him, unless you just happened to be looking for him and you knew what he was driving. The beautiful sunlight had dripped away giving way to a dark night sky. Only a subtle orange presence remained in the distance, the last fading light of the day. Tony found and pulled into a parking space, that said parents of the football players. For just a moment he sat at on his bike processing everything. He tried to calm down and breathe. The sweat that Tony had felt was gone, all gone. The feeling of being on fire with it. It was almost as if he had been baptized on his journey to the football field. He could not explain what he was feeling. His breathing slowed and he became calm. Sounds of cheering fans, laughter and people just having a great time began to register in his mind. As a parent, he was familiar with these sounds from the times that he'd drop John off at football practice or from the few times he'd pick him up from school in the past. Everything about it felt normal. Though he was still slightly alarmed by his possible lost time incident. He took note that he physically felt different. Tony slowly removed his biker helmet. Even the sweat he felt inside the helmet was gone. A weird chill ran up his spine. He knew it and he did not have to say it, yet he did not want to admit it to himself, at least not yet. He'd wait until he gathered all the facts and information before coming to any conclusion. He would just keep it as a noted thought in the back of his head. He would not share it with anyone. The helmet was placed on the top of the bike near one of the handle bars where it hung off the edge. Even though the bike was a bit aged, it still looked like an American Masterpiece. It was brilliant in all its faded glory, yet finite in its excellence. The bike was getting its share of the attention. People walked by it, staring at its shine and whistling, admiring and handing out compliments to Tony about his hog as if they were candy. The very moment Tony stepped off the bike, he felt it. A tugging sensation. As if his center of gravity was off. He'd never felt anything like this in his entire life physically. Briefly his entire world was shaking, quaking as if to say something had been instilled within him, carefully and thoughtfully, but what? Everything was spinning. He vomited every bit of the pizza up that he had eaten earlier. The passersby, who were family, teachers, and students noticed.

"Mr. Cheverie, are you alright?" a student asked.

A teacher in the area came to Tony's aid. A beautiful woman with black hair walked up to Tony.

"Care for some help?" the sweet-sounding voice asked.

Tony looked up and he swore he'd seen and angel. The woman's hands were in a way reached out towards him.

"I am Ms. Dorman, one of the school nurses. Would you like a towel to clean the vomit and a Gatorade to replenish yourself, or would you prefer water?" Ms. Dorman asked.

He stood there for a moment with vomit draining from his lips, falling into the puddle below. He was used to having the upper hand in nearly every situation in his life. Tony was not used to being in such a vulnerable position, especially in front of someone so beautiful.

"Yes please. Gatorade," Tony replied taking the offer gracefully and without regret.

He wiped the mess from his face, mouth and shirt. He was quite relieved that he'd gone to the lake wearing civilian attire. The last thing he needed was to send a pair of khakis to the cleaners with vomit stains. The woman handed Tony a Gatorade after he cleaned himself up. He snapped it open. And yet another thing he noticed. His body did not need the drink. He thought perhaps with all of the sweating that he'd done within the last ten to thirty minutes, that the drink would taste as sweet as Kool-Aid, not so. It was as sour as it could possibly be. Another chill ran up Tony's spine, yet he relented and went into the other direction with his thoughts trying to concentrate on something in the here and the now.

"Ms. Dorman is it?" Tony asked as if trying to play it off nonchalantly.

The woman perked up a bit to his manners and her smile grew almost a thousand miles wide.

"Have you heard from John? I've been trying to call him for the past few hours with no luck. Could you point me in the direction of where he might be? Some answers would help," Tony asked in a bit of a worried voice.

The woman smiled and pointed over at the football field which by now was completely lit up and the sun already escaped the sky without a warrant to stay.

One thing Tony immediately noticed as he walked closer to the field from the parking lot. Across the street from the practice field was the playing field, which was a massive stadium the lights were on there as well. Students were running back and forth, but there were also large bright lights on the practice field as well. Ms. Dorman walked with Tony over to the practice field. The only sight to

104

see was the equipment crew dragging shoulder pads and balls off the field.

"What am I looking for? Where is John?" asked Tony.

The school nurse looked lost for a second.

"I thought that they were still over here. They all must have gone over to the stadium. They kept saying they might try the new plays on the big field when it got dark, but everybody was unsure because they'd already run two practices today," added Ms. Dorman.

While Tony had been preoccupied with talking to Ms. Dorman and trying to find John, Roman's blue SUV, with a slightly changed body style and out of state tags rolled into the parking lot. Tony never even noticed the guy, nor did the vehicle look out of place. Roman even had a disguise in hand ready, as a lost tourist. As he was parked in the lot with all the other random vehicles. He deployed the drone again, which first checked out the practice field, where nothing just happened to be happening.

"Where's the action at sweetheart?" Roman was essentially saying to the drone.

The sun had gone down and it was dark. There was a slight chance that the drone would appear over the field as an anomaly, so that best thing Roman could do was film from either end zone at a particular height but well zoomed in. This was all to avoid being caught in the middle of the action by anyone possibly filming the practice. Because there was always that outside chance that someone's hand held MiniDV would pick up the mysterious glare of a top secret invisible government spy drone. There was always that chance. Tony and Ms. Dorman walked through the stadium entrance. It was massive. The smell was the first thing to hit you, the grass. They were surrounded by huge concrete pillars on all sides, but there was also an immense amount of technology all around them showing updates of the game and such.

Tony rushed onto the field where he saw John and his teammates having a great time running plays. Ms. Dorman invited Tony to sit next to her on the teacher's bench.

"Won't this look a bit odd, a parent sitting with the school faculty?" Tony asked.

"Don't you worry. It will all be alright," Ms. Dorman replied.

Before his father's eyes, John began to do things on the field that his father had never seen him do, much less anybody else. There were ooohs and ahhhs from the crowd. It was like John was not only a better football player but a different one as well. His arm strength, his ability to read the defense and even to run the ball, everything about his game had improved, but how? Tony could hear the questions around him. He heard a man whispering 'USO incident' to another old woman, Tony quite frankly wanted to get up and tell the old busy bodies to mind their own business, but he knew drawing any attention was not helpful. Everything was going great on the field.

John was showing that he was a surefire talent, before he had a shot to go to whichever school he wanted. And a few NFL scouts were even on hand. One was slowly making his way over to the direction of Tony. The scout was from the Patriots. Tony had never really gotten into any one team as a fan, though he did enjoy the game in general. The scout walked up to Tony's section and asked to sit and watch, and they allowed the scout to sit. An attempt was made at small talk between the scout and Tony, but the scout was more interested in taking notes of the talented young man and what he could do on the field. Tony noticed he was being asked almost empty questions about his son, everything had to do with football. Tony obliged but knew the conversation would go nowhere. That those people did not have his best true interests at heart. For a brief second, Chief Cheverie turned away from the field. John threw an interception to the "opposing side", which happened to be that schools defense. John did the impossible and ran the defensive back down, tackling him and in the process taking him to the ground in a violent manner. The defensive back took offense to the situation at hand. He shoved John. John shoved back. A brawl occurred between the two on the field. John hit his fellow senior so hard that his football helmet flew off and the young man flew back off the ground six to ten feet behind him. The scout who just watched this marvel occur, slowly turned over Tony with a smile, as if he'd seen a god grace the gridiron.

"We'll be in touch," the Scout said as he shook Tony's hand with glee and handed him the team's business card.

Some people on the field were yelling and booing John, others cheering him. The fight died down and John left the field. Of the students surrounding him, they did not know if they should congratulate him or run away. They all knew the same thing that Tony did. Something was not quite right with his son. He'd never seen him play that well. It was only since the Mile Marker 9 incident that he's been this damn good. So, it was then that the thought flowed through Tony's mind that something really did happen to them all that day, something that changed their lives forever to each one of them. He firmly believed that without question now. And every single bit of what happened had just been caught on tape by the invisible drone that Agent Roman had deployed above the stadium. The Agent could not believe his eyes, that everything he'd just seen had actually happened. Something was afoot in the town of Eastport. Roman was making a connection essentially that Tony had some sort of relationship with the USOs as did possible his friends and family, especially his son, from the footage he just saw. The very moment that his son hit the other player, the drone detected an elevated measurement of electromagnetic/ kinetic discharge coming from John's body. Basically meaning his son possibly had some sort of hidden kinetic gift about himself, drawn out by his experience that nobody had realized. But the only ones who knew for sure now about this were Agent Roman, and the government because of the invisible drone's footage.

Before Tony left the Stadium, he felt really sick again. He had to throw some water on his face. As he walked towards the restroom he noticed a man wearing a hat, black glasses and tourist attire following him.

"Who wears black glasses this time of the night?" he thought.

He kept walking and lost the desire to care why, or even who the man was. Tony entered the bathroom and began to run the water, throwing it on his face, hands, arms, and neck. Agent Roman entered the bathroom. He was wearing a sophisticated wire, a very tiny one in his ear that could pick up any conversation within one hundred yards according to the wearer's preference. When Tony saw the man enter the restroom, he didn't think much of it.

"So what. Another guy needing to use the can," Tony thought.

As he took his wrist watch off to wash his wrists as well, he tried not to pay any attention to the man in glasses. It was only then when he dropped his watch and went to pick it up, that the man wearing the glasses was standing right next to him where he was kneeled. The man looked down at him and aggressively grabbed Tony's collar picking him up with great strength, dragging him over near the wall.

"We know that the girl is an alien. And we know that she talked to you about her undersea home base," Agent Roman said.

Tony falls to his knees begging, and pleading for what he was not sure. He kept saying, 'I didn't know.' Over and over again, while he wept. His hands covered his face as he was on his knees in mental anguish. When he opened his eyes, the man with the glasses was gone. Tony was feeling completely overcome with fear, so much to the point that he could not even begin to control it. He left the restroom in haste and the team was just leaving the field. Practice and showing off had been a done deal for the day. Tony let John know that he was heading home because he did not feel well. John said he would be headed that way very soon as well. Tony got onto his bike and made a quick trip of it to his house. He could not get over everything that had transpired that day. When John came home, his dad was passed out on the couch. John helped himself to the rest of the Pizza and the young hungry football player even raided the fridge. That night the weather got bad. For once the rain fell with a fury. The forecast showed that it was to be like this for at least the next two weeks. An odd weather system was moving through the area. When Tony finally dozed off, his body was completely numb. The first thing he saw was a white flash. The girl, Eleanor, was in his dream. He could not tell what she was saying. She was just pointing towards the underwater alien home base. Another flash, and Tony was suddenly on one of the USOs underwater somehow. He was on a platform, laying down. He saw his motorbike in the corner suspended in animation, standing still yet going its constant speed and stuck in some sort of time bubble. They began to speak to Tony.

"We saw you get into the underwater device with the young lady and the older man. We watched you as you viewed the locations of our peaceful underwater dwellings. Do you plan on harming us the same way that your military does?" Alien Leader Ohm asks.

The dream state was quite vivid. Tony laid on the couch like a child having a nightmare during a storm. He had a crooked, yet sad and scared look on his face. As he spoke in his dream, he uttered the words with his lips.

"No, I would never do this to you. I am trying to help. You all can trust me. I am here to only help you," Tony replied in the dream to the vivid Alien Leader Ohm.

Ohm and the others walk into a corner and huddle for a moment and then they agree that they can trust Tony. Ohm also whispers something else in his ear and says, "You will remember this also when the time is right."

And then another white flash occurs. Tony awakens just after two am to a text message from Captain McGurk.

"Sleeping well? Enjoy it while you can. We attack at dawn."

Chief Cheverie jumps out of bed with a nervous frenzy about himself, ready to do what he'd set out to do, help the aliens all while appearing to help the government.

Now that Tony knew he'd been followed, he did everything in his power to make certain he was not being followed any more. There was always the drone, but it had not been put on him that day. Apparently, there was already enough evidence on Tony to put him away for a long time for treason against humanity and the United States Government by helping the aliens.

Tony figured, "What the hell do I have to lose now?"

He ventured over to the lake and ended up meeting some of the aliens, by chance. One of which was a leader of theirs named Ohm, whom he had already met before.

"You remember us, me?" asked the leader.

"Vaguely. Look things are about to get here in a few hours, around dawn or so. If you need a place to stay I have an area that you can hide safely in. It's an old, World War 2 bunker in the lower part of my house. Nobody will find you there."

"Thank you for the offer Tony Cheverie. You are a great human being, but we must try to weather this struggle alone. Perhaps if our races reach a peace accord, we can try to work with you side by side, but until then, we must tend to our underwater dwellings. Your government and military intends to attack us within hours," Ohm said.

"I understand, and I will try to continue to help you all in any way that I possibly can," Tony replied in a sorrow filled voice.

Tony stares out at the body of water near his house. He can see the flicker of sunrise cracking over the edge of the horizon. War has finally come home with him. Tony had to hurry to get to his post as well, to keep appearances up. He arrived at the dock just in time to climb aboard his ship with the rest of the crew.

Episode 10: Warfare

The Navy is set up on water and underwater to fight. The aliens fight back with weapons they created to disintegrate the military weaponry. Alien homes underwater are being destroyed left and right. They had to call for help from an alien friend from outer space.

The Navy had amassed a presence not seen since the 1940's in the area. The threat of the USOs and the location of their bases was being taken as a serious threat to National Security and to the preservation of the United States of America. Humanity itself was on high alert with all of the hysteria in the media. Orders had come in to gather as many ships and crew as possible to assemble immediately. The plan was to strike the location of the aliens' underwater home bases and to destroy as many of them as possible. Battleships, aircraft carriers, and submarines, everything was brought together.

It was also making the rounds on the news as something big was coming about, but the military was playing it off as war games to be ready for any and all threats known to mankind. It was all hands-on deck. War was on the table, and they were all at death's doorstep banging their fists on the door with their cannons locked and loaded no matter the consequences. The time was 1 am when the order came in. The ships had already gotten underway. Torpedoes had been locked into place, even a few nuclear warheads were on the submarines just in case they needed some real firepower against the aliens. All of the commanding Officers and ship's Captains were briefed on the matter, and they basically had to be a bit mum with their crew about what exactly they were doing. They were not allowed to view the media at any time that day, that was a fleet wide black out, but at the same time each crew was told a different reason for the fleet build up. It was everything from war games, to doing 'active,' dry run exercises. To looking to 'stimulate' dangerous yet rare sea life that had not been seen in thousands of years, which was expected to rise from the depths of the ocean to attack humanity. All sorts of rumors began to float among the crew members. All they knew for sure was they had an attack on their hands. It tasted like war, fear and death rolled all into one. And to them, it tasted good. Some of them had never seen any live action. And others it had been way too long since they'd seen any. They were chewing at the bit to destroy something, anything. A message came across the Grinder's Emergency Action Message Network. Grinder was the nickname of the submarine. Its official Naval call sign however was SS-160.

"Captain we have an urgent Emergency Action Message," the First Officer said as he gave the printed paper to the Captain.

The Captain, Captain Fisher, took the paper and read it aloud to the code man with the key, who unlocked a safe which confirmed the message to launch when ordered to with a signal. The Captain put the launch key around his chest, as did the First Officer. The Grinder had been put on red alert.

Submarine Sonar Officer Haynes stared at the green circular screen intensely. The young man was all of twenty-two years of age. He was scared, yet ready to give his life for his country and all of humanity. The crew had a general idea of just what they were doing there, but they did not know the whole story.

"Captain Fisher, what did you say we were looking for again? Renegade psychopathic whales?" First Officer Samson asked with a chuckle.

"We are looking for an underwater species that does not belong in the area. We have been told to destroy its habitat if we discover any sign of its existence or life in the immediate area," Captain Fisher replied.

He was towing the intelligence communities line. It was obvious. The Captain knew what they were looking for, possible alien underwater bases, or the aliens themselves. He was briefed on the matter in an intelligence meeting earlier, though it's not like he could just come out and tell his crew "Oh, hey we're alien hunting," because who knows what type of panic such a thing would instill within one's crew.

Things like that are what mutinies are made of. The green screen was empty. It was there to find large objects showing up. There was also a larger green sonar map, set up on the bridge near the charting station on the submarine. If anything came up on the small submarine, it would show up on that screen with more detail, but only to whomever was wearing specific goggles which provided detailed information of the object or objects in question being detected by sonar.

Tony had settled in on his ship. He was the Science Officer on board. Just as he was coming on board, his Commanding Officer briefed him on the situation even though he already knew what was going on.

"Chief, we received some stingy intelligence early in the am to suggest some unfriendly species were gathered and ready to wage war against us under the water. We were told that you had been doing extensive work and research outside of the U.S.S. Barrow," First Officer Hammond said.

"Yes Sir. I was contacted and assigned to the project and asked to look over and apply myself with all of my knowledge. I thoroughly researched and analyzed everything that was collected beforehand and then I came to many conclusions, which I then submitted to Captain McGurk of the United States Army," Tony replied.

"Yes, we saw the report. It's good to have someone on your side who knows what they are doing, and how exactly to defeat the enemy," Hammond added.

Out on the deck while the First Officer and Tony were finishing the briefing up, a Private who was manning the artillery on their battleship scoured the lake ocean surface for any odd activity. It was like a fisherman waiting for the fish to bite. Only these fish would be much larger, about the size of city bus if not larger, and the bait just happened to be torpedo's, stinger missiles, and tomahawk missiles. The Navy was not going to hold back. Based on all of the intelligence that was received, they were going all in. They meant to eradicate this underwater infestation before they could spread any further. A subtle shiny object poked above the splashing of the water. As the Private stared into the eyepiece of the mounted artillery gun. He straightened his sound dampening headphones to protect his ears during blasts. He looked into the viewfinder concentrating on the shiny object. His eyes got huge when he saw it was something that should not be there. And it was not just some rogue animal species or even what they'd been told during their briefings. It was something not of this world. The Private fired off the first shot in the battle. The small recon USO was immediately destroyed, causing a huge blast to occur and it had drawn the attention of the entire fleet as well as the aliens below the sea who were trying to become more prepared to defend their homes or possibly to fight and escape if need be. One after another the ships, all of them. The other battleships, aircraft carriers began to fire. The voice of Captain McGurk rang out over the radio.

"Who gave the order to fire?" McGurk asked in an annoyed tone.

At first McGurk was annoyed but then he quickly accepted the situation because this is exactly what he wanted, war and to destroy these things. Tony was ordered to the bridge to assist with giving orders to the other sailors and with anything on the deck that was needed by the artillery men. He was also sent across the ship checking pressure and temperature gauges to make certain the aliens would not try to malfunction their ship in any way that might be out of the ordinary. He was to try to detect anything that was out of their ability to defend themselves with. Tony was asked to be on watch for anything peculiar happening that could not be explained. Such things were not told to the rest of the crew. If they knew word-for-word what the briefings were all about ... the possibly of a war and hand to hand combat with alien creatures that were living in the ocean and surrounding lakes of the area, then the crew would lose their own sanity. The scene was one for the ages, bombs going off in every direction, most of the explosions were occurring underwater. There were underwater Naval diving mini-subs to gather intel during the battle, so much death and destruction was taking place. All of the alien dwellings within the lake's area were nearly destroyed. The Navy had not reached much of the inhabited ocean area's yet where the alien bases were.

McGurk was screaming from the deck of the ship that he was stationed on. He had sort of been given permission to commandeer a

Naval Destroyer. Even though they were in different branches of the US Armed Forces, McGurk had been handed the Command of the Entire fleet. Officer Haynes, stared at his screen. The tooth pick which had been poking out of the corner of his mouth, dropped like a lone pin hitting the floor.

"Captain Fisher, Sir! Look!" Haynes said.

The Captain hurried over to the submarine officer's radar screen. Both of them watched as the entire screen lit up.

"What is it?" Captain Fisher asked.

"It's big, whatever it is," Haynes replied.

A large sound was heard looming overhead and all around them. The sound grew and expanded so much to the point that the men on the sub covered their ears. It was like a loud annoying echo with a shallow yet screeching effect to it, and then it went all hollow like a massive moan from deep in the water. Haynes was listening to the sonar and even though everyone else could not hear the terrifying sound that all across the submarine had just heard with their ears did not mean that the sound had stopped. The young submarine officer heard the sound as if something was rotating, and or possibly reloading.

He yelled. "Brace for it. Hold something they are going to fire some sort of weapon," Haynes said.

He was a smart young man. Captain Yunel of the USS Esquire, and Captain Ren of the USS Spike watched on carefully from their bridges, awaiting further orders.

"Hey, do you see this light that is emanating from deep in the ocean?" Captain Yunel asked.

"We can see the same thing over here at the lake," another ship's Captain replied.

It was a massive green light that was ascending from deep in the water. The water had a medium blue color to it. It was not overly polluted, yet it was not the type of water you would simply just go dip glasses in and drink raw without being processed first. The green glowing grew and grew with more chatter flowing over the open radio.

"Do you see it? What is it?" Captain Yunel asked.

Without anytime or sign other than the ever-growing light, two ships were suddenly blasted by a powerful beam green beam of what seemed to be laser light from the water. It was the same green glowing light that had been seen by Captain Yunel and the other ship commanded by Captain Stevens over in the lake area.

Ren just watched on in horror. There were so many things he wanted to say. He was quiet and still quiet again until just before the moment that it happened.

The words ... "God have mercy on our souls," were said by Captain Ren over the USS Spikes ship wide intercom.

The light became more than a beam. A smell was noticed. It was a burning smell. Steam was seen all around and over the two ships. Captain Yunel was in a panic. His crew was trying everything they could to stop whatever this green stuff was that was bursting out at them from underneath the water below.

"Captain, we don't know what this is, but it's causing all controls to malfunction. Sir, we are getting all sorts of strange readings on board. Everything from temperature to pressure gauges are going haywire. Captain!!" three different crew members yelled.

Captain Yunel was losing his own marbles. He'd never been in such a haunted situation in all his years commanding the Esquire. His ship began to get warmer. Everyone began to sweat more and more. They complained that their skin was on fire. Their heartbeats were racing a thousand miles a minute. Radio comms were down. They tried to hail the other ships for some type of help, but no radio signals were going out or coming in now. They could not however, get over the intense burning smell in the air. Everything from the rubber, to the iron, to hair and human flesh, filled the air around them with a burning odor. The men and the women of the ship Esquire began to panic. Whatever this process that they were going through seemed as if it were hours long worth of agony and pain. Some people tried to drink water and eat food. Everything had lost its taste. The clocks on the ship had stopped at just after dawn, the time that the attacks on the aliens had commenced that morning. A vague green bubble surround each of the two ships. Little if any movement of other ships or submarines was noticed from their bridge or their ships decks. Nothing could be detected on the radar screens. They were like sitting ducks in the water.

However, something was occurring. It was unexplainable, other than the odd symptoms and things that were being reported across the ship. Crew members kept saying that they had tried to eat and drink, but that everything had lost its taste. Other people said that their bodily functions had ceased. More and more crew members were being admitted to the sick bay of both ships. One by one they were reporting of having their organs shut down. Everything from dehydration to renal failure, to brain death, and severe seizures were occurring in droves on the ship without control. The only cause that could be considered was the green haze/ bubble that had consumed the ship hours ago when all of the instruments went haywire and all of the ship's power went down. The weirdest part was, it was as if a day had passed. Most of the crew began to break down mentally. Some ran around wearing just bras and panties or their boxer briefs as if totally mad. Others wanted to test the theory of what would happen if they jumped off the ship into the water. The Captains on each ship paid attention to this carefully. A handful of sailors from each ship tried the crazy idea. The men and women immediately evaporated when their bodies touched the water. They practically melted before the eyes of their own crew members who watched on in horror. All of them knew that they were next. Captain Yunel's eyes began to hurt, as did the others. Their eyes, ears, noses, orifices began to bleed all over their body. One by one the crew began to hemorrhage violently. A young lady who was a sailor ran through the mess hall screaming, when she dropped to the floor. A small group went into the room to check in on her. They found her skull had popped open from all of the pressure. Her brains were splattered all over the mess hall floor. She wasn't alone. Other crew members experienced this, exploding hearts, and sudden strokes. The symptoms were getting worse and the bodies were piling up. The air itself that they were breathing began to burn. It was not just every breath that they were taking, but they could feel it on their skin as well as if hot pricks like pens were poking them. And along with this they looked at the green haze that surrounded the ship. The green was becoming brighter, almost shining in front of the crew members and the Captain on the deck of the Esquire. Screaming was heard all over the ship. People were dropping like flies. The light became bright and intense exactly at the same time that things around the crew began to melt. Sudden fires erupted and the crew members themselves erupted into spontaneous fires, some blowing up on the spot sending their flesh in multiple directions. It was not much longer until finally all of the energy that was combusting on the two small ships finally exploded from the green blast that came from below. The situation that the crews on the ships the USS Esquire and the USS Spikes seemed to them to happen over a period of some twenty plus hours, but it still seemed as if it was just after dawn the same morning that the attack started. However to everyone else watching on, as this green haze enveloped the two ships, it all happened in a manner of about ten or twenty minutes. At the moment, they disintegrated pieces of tiny matter scattered hundreds of thousands of feet. They were so small that it could not be told what was what. It was more like tiny grains of sands scattering on the wind. The ships and crews watching on didn't even hear any screams. It was a sight that no one would ever forget.

McGurk immediately ordered all ships to open fire with everything that they had on the area in which the green blast came from. It's not like they would run out of missiles or artillery. They'd packed enough weaponry to kick off a war with a country, or even perhaps World War 3. All of the submarines, even the one which had sustained heavy damage from USO blasts while submerged, began to fire everything they had at the green burst which came from under the water. The radio techs and radar officers on every ship and submarine began to focus and work together. Losing one of their own, really pissed off the Navy. And it happened right before their very eyes. There was technically nothing that they could even do about the entire thing. It happened so fast to them, yet unknowingly so slow to the crews who died on the two ships.

"Captain, that's one, two, three torpedoes off," Haynes said.

"Good, get 'em, Whatever the hell they are, we're gonna send 'em back with a postage stamp that says, don't fuck with the United States Navy," Captain Fisher replied.

Torpedoes and missiles in bunches were tearing apart the underwater dwellings of the aliens. Tony watched on in overwhelming sadness as there was nothing that he could do, other than go about what he was supposed to do, to look as if he was doing his job. Pieces of alien ships and even some alien bodies were floating in the water. The crew members on the remaining ships became distraught.

"Oh my ... is that what I think that is?" asked one radio tech.

Captain McGurk immediately went out over the radio to all ships.

"Disregard what you are seeing in the water. They are not peaceful. They are here with hostile intentions. They mean to destroy us. We are the saviors of mankind. We will prevail," McGurk said as his voice echoed across all of the ships and submarines as every man and woman who was fighting in the fleet that day realized the full scope of the event that they were involved in that day.

At first the feeling among the crew members was hurt from losing everyone on the two ships and then it was complete and utter chaotic violence, well nauseated, yet climatic fear. And then they all felt an odd sense of accomplishment and pride. That they had stood toe to toe with the alien creatures and destroyed those who had destroyed their fellow crew members, who had just paid the ultimate price moments ago. The missiles and torpedoes continued. Sonar Officer Haynes notified his Captain that a strange sound was emitting from the alien bases from below. It was some type of signal. The beam of the signal was powerful, yet not the same type that just destroyed the two ships.

"Captain, I think it's either a homing beacon of some sort or a distress call," Haynes added.

THE TRIUMPH

Episode 11: Power or Life

Tony is injecting the aliens with a substance that will camouflage the alien's blood to appear human so that they are not caught and killed. The alien's friend from outer space showed up and the tide turns overwhelmingly in the favor of the aliens.

The footsteps are brutal and defined. They carry with them meaning and purpose. An attempt to stave off a war that could destroy mankind and even possibly new-found allies from another world. Tony was running about across the ship, checking gauges and helping whom he could as he was told, when the idea came to him. He kept tight lipped about it because with such a thing he could trust nobody on the boat, but he could trust one man to help buy him some time in order to do what needed to be done. Tony enlisted one of the sailors under his immediate command to take care of most of his tasks. He went to First Class Sailor Jason Simons. Simons was from Alabama. He was a good ole boy. A big stocky guy with a southern accent that couldn't be missed. He made a list of things that were needed to be done all so that he could concentrate on creating a substance that will camouflage the alien's blood. The idea is that essentially this substance will make the aliens appear to be human, so that they can hide. Also that they are not caught or killed.

"Simon, I've got some important things to take care of. Would you mind taking care of this list of items I wrote down?" Tony asked.

Tony handed the small binder to the hulk of a man that Simon was. His big eyes and stubby fingers to match looked over the book as if it was something he'd never seen before.

"Chief, this ain't my job. But, I'd be more than happy to help ya. Would you put a special word in with the cook of the ship to sees about getting fresh cornbread and spare ribs on the next dinner menu?" asked Simon.

"Why sure, anything for you Simon," replied Tony. Simon, being the extremely big, tall, and strong fella that he was. Even though he could practically intimidate the side of a battleship with his brow or even bend backwards any piece of steel with the flicker of his giant looking fingers, his one weakness was food. Don't let him fool you though. Some people think the big man is slow, and a complete idiot. He pays attention though. You give him orders and directions, he follows them to a T, and gets them done precisely and timely like an expert.

Simon began to thumb through the binder. The pages were marked with markers and highlighted yellow sticky notes. Every single gauge that Tony had to check, and area that he had to go into to help reload cannons or bullet cartridges for deck guns. All of the information was there.

"Now remember Simon, if the Captain of the boat, or anyone asks where I am. You tell them I am working on a poison to kill the alien's with," Tony added.

Simon had a sort of an empty stare look on his face. As if his mind was already drifting towards the cornbread and ribs.

"Simon, what did I just say?" Tony asked.

Simon's head froze for a moment because his nose had been eyebrow deep in the binder that Tony just gave him.

"Ugh,... you said ugh something about aliens," Simon replied.

Tony scoffed, and sort whispered to himself a rhetorical question. "What are we going to do with you Simon?"

"I don't know but it better involve cornbread and ribs," Simon replied with a chuckle.

Tony took a small notepad from his back pocket and a black ink pen from his side. He scribbled something on it really quick.

"Here this is what I want you to say," Tony added.

Tony wrote on the note to tell them I am making a poison to kill the Aliens, and that I am not to be disturbed. I will try to finish as soon as possible to help us win this war and to destroy the aliens for once and for all. Tell them that I had an idea on how to stop the alien menaces."

Tony wrote a note to really sell it good. Simon read the note and agreed to pass the message along to whomever. The young man from Alabama was now locked in, and ready to proceed with his new orders.

Tony steadily marched towards his lab. He climbed down a handful of familiar ladders from deck to deck to bring him to the hallway adorned with posters that made soldiers feel more at home while on the ship. His eyes gazed at the metal door with the rounded wheel turning lock on it. It said, *Chief Cheverie* in big bold letters. He wound the wheel counter clockwise and the door opened, of course with the loudest of aching springs in desperate need of oil. Tony walked into the enclosed space carefully closing the metal door with the wheeled lock on it behind him. His eyes beamed down to the lock, as if paranoid of someone barging in on him to discover what they may be up to next. Immediately he placed the lock on the metal door.

"Nobody would be able to get in without him allowing it. I can now work in peace and accomplish something great," Tony thought.

The echos from above and to the side of bomb's doing off all around during the battle, as well as the sounds of sailor's screaming. Word of a fire on the ship was actually what got Tony's nerves jumping, because if the ship went down, or up in flames all his work would be lost in the private lab on his ship. And thus would be an end to him trying to help the alien's. All would be lost, and a war would have been started for sure, something well out of the confines of this harbor, and this city. Tony knew that if the fight grew beyond this area, that it would be the end of the alien's, and quite possibly mankind.

A computer and a table of chemicals, stood between mankind and the alien's that the humans were now firing upon in the battle that had broken out. Tony opened the operating system to his classified computer, entering his password and bringing up the database that all of his research was stored in. He selected the necessary files, reading the contents and then applying said information to the chemical's he had on hand. Along with all of this he had tiny samples of alien

125

blood, bodily fluids and skin. He needed these things to synthesize a 'blocker' that would start a chemical reaction within the aliens' blood, thus making them appear human. The military had apparently developed a new technology that Tony had not been aware of until just now, which could detect the alien's according to a chemical signature in their blood. Tony isolated it, and figured out a way to 'mask' it, thus the need for the 'blocker'. Tony made enough of the 'blocker' for the aliens to make their own and distribute it properly. He had no real way of showing the alien's how to create more. His best bet was to give the aliens the samples he created. And a portion of his own human DNA and blood samples. The ship took a major hit. It began to tilt a small amount and water began to rush in from the floor. At first it was drops, and then it started to steadily grow from there. Tony knew that he had to get the hell out of there, but he also knew that he could would likely lose every piece of his research and physical inventory that he'd use to fall back onto. He packed a waterproof container that had a chain and lock on it, the combination to which he only knew. In this container, he would put into it, not only all of his copies of all his research files from the database but also all of the physical samples that could not be recreated, as well as the cloned samples. And physical files that were also needed for later purposes, and not to mention anything that could later tie him back to the helping the aliens later on. So, in essence, not only was he saving all data that could destroy the aliens, but all of the data to save them as well. Leaving either one felt wrong. And it's as if something just kept saying... "You will regret it later if you don't save all of the samples and all of the information." So he did.

The ship was sinking. And to think Tony had been worried about how to find a way off the ship quietly to help the alien's, without being seen as missing or having gone AWOL. This was Tony's perfect opportunity. During the process in which Tony was creating the 'blocker', a large ship appeared in the sky. It was so large that it filled up the entire scene of the battle with plenty of room to be seen. A large unidentified humming sound was heard just before the ship entered the atmosphere of planet Earth. When the ship descended from the sky to hover just over the battle, it caught many off guard. The ship went on what seemed to be forever. Its shadow loomed over the ship's. Sailors, marines alike looked up to the sky not knowing what to think other than impending fear. Their eyes were locked upon this great towering infinity that made them feel small and suddenly insignificant. Some of the men's lives began to flash before their very eyes. They knew that this was their end though they were not ready to die. Some of the soldiers and sailors panicked, but very few. A majority of the men and women were ready to lay their lives down to die for humanity. Even if it meant they stood no chance against the shadowy menace that lingered above them. For a brief moment, they all stared up above at it. The flurry of canon's blasting and laser beams that shot from the water to damage the ships, all seemed to come down to small isolated incidents. There was this sneaky, yet creepy quiet all about the battle scene. The air stood still, the stench of death had already begun to make its presence known, both below and above the waterline of the bodies of water. Large laser beams were fired from the ship, one at a time upon the larger ships first. No longer did they soldiers and sailors concentrate their fire on the water, but on the sky to take this thing out.

"Take that sonofabitch down," one sailor said with fear in his voice.

Captain McGurk chimed in. "Give it everything we've got and more, we're almost there boys. We've got this!"

Little did the Captain or the fleet know that even though they had been monitoring communications for quite some time now, the aliens had managed to send out a secret signal to one of their friends, a distress signal is what some might call it. They put out the message that they were in grave danger that the inhabitants of Earth were hostile. And they included that the people of Earth meant to do them harm and had attacked them, killing many of their race, that peace was not an option here. They told their friends that Earth wanted war only, but with the only ending being death of everyone and everything on the planet. And now the shadowy object now loomed over the battle scene firing laser's down on the ships, which began to sink from said actions.

Tony ran through the halls of the ship. Water rushed under his feet. At first it was mere inches. Now it was bucketsful of water flowing past his own walking two. He sloshed with each step. It was becoming more and more difficult to move within the ship and drag this large waterproof container with its chain. Tony looked and saw a life preserver, and he looked at his metal container. For a moment, he felt he was going to half to make a tough decision, his own life, and wearing it and floating, or pretending that he drowns and going down to the bottom to help save the aliens immediately and stopping the battle. He shook off the preserver, and went for the next best option, one of the Navy's most sophisticated scuba diving suits along with a mini sub for two people. He also took a two-way radio to listen in on the fleet themselves. Tony looked into the launch bay and half of the mini subs were destroyed. The Chief figured, well maybe this one won't go unmissed and I can actually get away with doing this. He loaded the metal container, chain and all into the sub. Basically the container would take up the weight of a second person, but without using the oxygen of a second person. When everything that he needed was in the mini sub, both his diving equipment and the metal container, he guided the mini sub off the edge of the slowly sinking ship. The Chief jumped down onto the sub which was now in the water far enough that it could submerge. He looked up into the sky and at the other ships. He looked around him at the utter destruction and of his own men dying. Tony heard cries all around him. The alien's powerful laser blasted the Navy's most mighty of ship's reducing them to mere crumb's. He witnessed as it's laser beam and its explosion filled up the sky, it stretched all the way down to the end of the coast line. The sense of dread within him that he was intense, one which he could not escape.

"Is this the end?" he wondered. And then Tony climbed up into the mini sub, after him tightly he shut the hatch above. The first thing he had to do was to pressurize when descending into the depths below. His ear's swelled up, as if a tiny balloon had just been activated in his own melon, his brain felt a sudden sense of pressure to it. On the sub with his daughter and her friend, Tony did not experience this. There was something special about this special prototype sub. It had a separate hatch and access point to leave the ship, and enter the ship with an extra pressurized hatch. And apparently from looking at the on-board sensor's he could go as low as 10,000 feet in the water and the hull of the mini sub would not crush. Usually the limit was between 2,000-4,000 feet and the hull would be crushed like a tin can from the pressure that far below the water.

With extreme caution Chief Cheverie made his way down to the depths where the alien's bases and ships were on the ocean floor, and in the lake where they had been parked.

There was just as much ruin, death, and destruction below the water as there was above the water. If it were not for the alien's friends arriving, the military would have annihilated the aliens, and quite possibly they would have still suffered a great many casualties in the process. But now that this extra-terrestrial friend had arrived the tide had been turned in the favor of the aliens. However, they still felt scared, afraid that mankind could muster the strength to destroy both them and their friends from outer space alike, quite swiftly.

Tony would attempt to quell those fears. Down below he saw a large bubble, the sub entered it. It was a weird experience, as soon as the sub entered the bubble it seemed void of gravity. The mini sub rested on a platform which the aliens had originally made for the humans to sat down on, if they wanted to peacefully correspond with the alien's and speak of peace, but as it would currently seem, that was not to be, or was it? When Tony arrived, he was not met with welcome arms. The aliens held devices that one would guess would be used for self-defense. They were simply straight rods with pointed beacons on the end. Their physical weapons were a cross between a spear and a laser rifle. The weapons were meant to stun and not kill, but if it were necessary, they would kill to protect themselves. However, they did not want to harm another living species, that was not their way. A group of aliens surrounded the sub ready to fire upon him. Another alien ran forward. He climbed out slowly with the metal container and his diving suit. He immediately saw that there were no water bubbles of air in the large bubbled arena win which he was encapsulated. A thought came to him, he closed his eyes.

"I'm either going to die or do something amazing."

He removed his diving helmet, and to his shock, pure and clean oxygen was within the bubble. Tony smiled. The one alien which had walked forward waved the others who were armed off. At first the alien spoke a weird language that Tony could not understand. It sounded like it was choking on pork chops. Its eyes got big and it seemed to be frustrated. It pushed a button on its wrist.

"There, is that better? My apologies, you must be Chief Cheverie, the human who was willing to work with us to attain peace. The brother of ours that you met with before was killed, others of us are not willing to work, but me and my crew are, at least most of us. Come aboard and let's see what we can do to end the death and the bloodshed," Alien Captain Kos said. Tony agreed and followed Captain Kos below into their ship, which was partially damaged, yet submerged thousands of feet below the water. As they walked they spoke some.

"Some of the other ships have been damaged worse than ours. We were lucky that some of our old friends answered a distress signal we sent out recently. We saw that your people were monitoring communications so we sent our version of what you'd call Morse Code," Captain Kos said.

Kos guided Tony into a large chamber, which appeared to be the combination of a scientist's lab and a medical operating room. As soon as he could Tony took the metal container and opened it. He took a small sample of what he had created and gave it to his counterpart on the alien ship. Kos reached his hand out, and shook Tony's hand.

"Thank you Mr. Cheverie we may have just prevented a war on this planet. Life may have been lost on this day, but all hope is not lost," Kos said.

"Hopefully we can get both sides to come to their senses and stop this idiotic fighting," Tony replied. The alien who was in charge of the lab quickly made extra samples of what Tony provided. The aliens quickly injected it and tested it next to Tony's blood. The onboard sensors showed that all of the aliens were appearing to be sensed as human beings. And hence this group of extraterrestrials,

130

from another world, looked at Tony as if he had been the savior of humanity. For a moment, Tony was going to give back every piece of research and sample he'd ever collected to the aliens. He didn't know where it came from or who, because the 'voice' that usually comes from Charlie has a distinct feeling about it. He just a had a feeling. Something said... 'don't'. So Tony decided to leave things as they were. Thus the aliens he'd just helped wanted to negotiate a peace with their brethren aliens to declare a ceasefire on humanity.

By this time, the onslaught had become great. Tony had gathered his things, gotten back into his diving suit, packed his metal container up, and got back into his mini-sub to head to the surface. When he reached the top, it was practically like a graveyard but with ships, and death all around. Very few ships and military submarines remained. The large alien ship above was firing its massive laser less and less often, though it still hovered overhead leaving all to think that there was no hope. Overheard on the radio that he packed was panic. Soldiers and sailors from all branches of the military were upset and totally losing it mentally. Tony knew immediately what needed to be done. He contacted Secretary Moss, and briefed him on everything.

"Sir, this is Chief Cheverie. I have an answer on how to get us out of this mess if you will allow me to," Tony said.

Moss answered with a sigh.

"We've lost great numbers of brave men and women and ships today, more than we thought we could have. Where were you with these answers days ago to prevent all of this?" Moss asked.

"That discussion is for another time, Sir. Right now the only time we have is to stop this. Do I have your permission?" Tony asked.

"If it brings about a peaceful cease fire in which we can somehow coexist with these aliens, or things or whatever they are then please by all mean's do what you think is best. And please brief me as soon as possible so that I mean brief the Joint Chiefs of Staff and the President of the United States personally. Somebody has got some explaining to do about all of this, because we may have started a battle under false pretenses," Moss added.

Captain McGurk was heard insulting his and other crews.

"All of you need to get the hell out of the way or just lay down and die. We won't give up this fight. This is our world not theirs!" added McGurk in an insane tone of voice.

A voice replied back on another ship.

"McGurk, we are all sitting ducks in the water. We've lost far too many crew members and ships. We are no match for them. If we continue this, we are likely to make things worse and even begin the annihilation of the human race."

There was a pause. McGurk was trying to find the words. He clicked his handheld radio.

"Look we can't quit, we have them---"

Cheverie rushes to the top and puts himself in harm's way physically by not properly depressurizing before opening the hatch. He felt a bit dizzy and nauseated when he came up. He'd heard enough of this jackass. He was going to put a stop to this right now! A very loud static sound is heard over the radio. Chief Cheverie's mini-sub is seen down in the middle of the water with his hatch open.

"You don't have to listen to this mad man anymore," Tony said.

"Who the hell just said that?" asked McGurk.

Everyone looked around and in the middle of the water among smoke and a damaged boat was Tony's mini-sub. McGurk looked around.

"Who the hell are you? Where the hell are you? How dare you!?"

The smoke cleared and, one-by-one, the Captains and their crews began to see Tony. When McGurk saw him, it angered him so much. He knew, he always knew, that Tony had been an extraordinary thorn in his side from day one. Whether out on the water for drills involving multiple branches, or even down at the Special Operations base.

"You son of a bitch. Its always been you every step of the way. You've always been the one loose end that I've had to think about. You people have no idea the things that I've had to do to keep us afloat, to win this fight. We can't leave. We can't pull out of this you cowards!" McGurk shouted.

Another voice, one calmer, the true voice of a leader that was level headed and objective interrupted.

"That will be quite enough Captain McGurk. Attention Fleet, this is Secretary Moss. The Secretary of the United States Navy. Disengage the enemy and cease fire until further notice. All ships, land vehicles and such raise your white flags. We are going to attempt to negotiate a peace with the alien beings, well at least Chief Tony Cheverie is going to," Moss added. McGurk loses it, he pushes the sailor at the controls for the tomahawk missiles out of the way.

"Enough of this shit!" McGurk yells in anger.

He blasts a missile towards Tony's direction. Narrowly missing him, but destroying his mini-sub, and the small already damaged boat next to him. The Chief barely escaped with his life. He was in the water with his metal container which was floating and his arms were draped over it. Moss became infuriated.

"I don't know how they do things in the Army McGurk, but here in the Navy, we have this thing called discipline."

McGurk still refused to surrender.

"You are not my commanding Officer you Navy Squid!" McGurk replied.

Tony knew that this back and forth would never end with McGurk and Moss. He knew they never really liked each other very much. He took it upon himself to do something, exactly as Moss said to do so. Tony confiscated another mini-sub and headed down to the aliens to get their attention.

Episode 12: Common Ground

Tony negotiates with the military captain on a deal so the killing of aliens will not be the policy of the military. Aliens present their proposal. The proposal is accepted. The negotiations make the news, and the aliens live in harmony with Earth-kind.

On his way back down into the dark depths of the ocean. Tony hears over the radio that McGurk was trying to surrender, and finally does. He was trying to pull his men out, but they were finding it difficult to escape with the large ship looming overhead. It's at this very moment that Tony hears McGurk over the radio blasting his name. "Cheverie get your ass back down in them depth's and order these aliens off of us!", said McGurk in a stern tone. Tony replied quickly, yet in an annoyed voice. "Roger Sir!" From there It felt like he was returning to a familiar and friendly place, it's as if he did not want to go back to the surface, but he knew that he had to. At the very moment he arrived they were waiting for him. "We've been listening, and we are ready to talk to your leaders.", said Kos the alien captain. This time he brought back a group of the aliens. They were leaders from each of the remaining alien ships, they were ready to negotiate a peaceful ceasefire. Not the surrender of humanity but for these alien's to somehow coexist. The desire was to come to a worthwhile understanding of each other, and to move forward in a harmonious fashion, that is best for both the extraterrestrial visitors and the people of Earth. Cheverie was told that in the coming week's both the leaders of humanity and the aliens that had been living in the waters on Earth for quite some time would sit down for formal peace negotiations. The aliens came to the surface as a sign of good faith to show their friends who traveled in the large ship in the sky that there was no more threat against them on Earth. Yet Tony and the other aliens went aboard the ship to negotiate everything, and thus an agreement was made. They thanked their friends but the ship still hovered over the battle site to insure the ceasefire and a forthcoming peace. The humans were allowed time to clean up and bury their dead, and tend to their wounded, as were the aliens. Pictures, video and interviews began to leak and surface of everything that went on during the battle. Leaders from both the human race and the extraterrestrials sat down at what would be known as landmark meeting. And at the very center of these proceedings was Chief Tony Cheverie. A time and a place had been chosen.

The trauma that had been experienced by the members of the military that day was nearly unfathomable. Mass hysteria in the streets was also occurring when the reports of the battle between the military and an armed extraterrestrial presence had broken out. It terrified and worried many. Many people were feeling leery about the peace talks. Others wondered why we did not finish the job and destroy the aliens. The public was quite split on the whole thing. People across the world believed that the world was coming to an end. Timing for the interviews of military members during the peace talks was actually not helpful at all, but the media chose to do so because it was trending like crazy at the moment. And they were right, the ad dollars rolled in like a runaway tsunami. Everyone from famous people to ordinary Joe's were asked their opinion on the entire matter. All types of reactions were recorded in the media. Who sipped the entire thing up like a bunch of naughty bloodhounds. There was no putting this cat back into the bag. During the cleanup process Charlie told Tony exactly what went on in town while he was away. "Everybody was losing their minds. One of them came on land in some suit. It was just me standing between this thing and Charlotte. We decided to go over to your house to keep John and Mabel company, we didn't know where else to go. So, we all just sorta hunkered down at your place. I hope that's alright Mr. Cheverie.", said Charlie. Tony nodded, while the two men were removing debris from the Chief's yard." Continue.", added Tony. "Oh, right, well there we were. Me and Charlotte, on the front porch in the rocking chairs, while Mabel and John boy were in the house were reading and watching football film. I had to protect the crew. And just with the way that my luck would have it. I heard this alien's thoughts. John left a shovel in the yard last week while doing his chores. And the alien freaked out when it saw the shovel." It was thinking. "Oh no, it's one of those oddly shaped metal things, those hurt I hope none of the Earthlings pick it up and try to harm me with it. Maybe they won't be smart enough to do so. Oh no it's one of the short one's with glass on its eyeball's, it's reaching for the metal thing.", thought the alien. "At this exact moment, I was running for the shovel and I grabbed it. I started to wave it around, I felt like a madman, thus swinging it at the alien and missing. It ran toward Charlotte and grabbed her as she stood in the doorway. Standing some twenty feet behind the alien who at that time had Charlotte held captive in its arms were Mabel and John. They watched on in horror as they thought they might be watching Charlotte's final moments alive.

The alien made funny choking and breathing sounds as if it was attempting to physically talk to or communicate with the young people. I knew exactly what it was trying to say." "If you come any closer the young earthling with the glass things on her eyeballs gets it.", added the alien. "John threw a clean football spiral at the alien, grabbing its attention long enough for me to run up and snatch Charlotte from the alien's grasp and to knock it on its feet with the shovel.", said Charlie. Tony shook his head with utter laughter. And then I said, "Unhand her you disgusting pig!", said Charlie. "So, it did not actually become apparent to your judgement until after everything, of what you had actually done right?", asked Tony. "Well of course, I had adrenalin running through my veins I could've stopped or picked up a city bus at that point.", laugh Charlie. "But you didn't, you thought things through quickly and you reacted quickly, thus you saved the day and showed what a real hero that you really are Charlie.", replied Tony. Charlie smiled at Tony. "You have to leave for the peace accord soon. And you are wanting me to go with you. Because there are things that you are not sure about, that you wish to keep between the two of us.", added Charlie. "Yes.", Tony replied in a quick but spooky manner. "Hey I can't help it, these things just come to me.", laughed Charlie. "There are just things that have happened and things that have come to me that me wonder if they were you, messages, to be careful basically.", added Tony. "I see.", said Charlie. Things got less silly and more serious. Charlie put on his serious face and went with Tony to the peace accord. And they were not alone that day. All of the news media outlets were there covering it. They were doing mini interviews of anyone and everyone leaving the place where the Peace Accord was being held, which just happened to be held on the football field where the team was playing football. A USO had emerged in the water next to the school, and a group of the alien leadership came out of the ship. Tony and Charlie as well as the military brass and an elite selection of politicians were on hand. Many people and aliens sat in the crowd. It was a great picture to behold and a mixture of a possible peaceful future to see of mankind and aliens alike getting along in absolute harmony. When the time came for the main parties to sit down, both Charlie and Tony were at the main negotiating table for Humanity along with the main leaders including McGurk and Moss. Kos was at the main negotiating table for the alien's along with the other leaders of the alien ships. Both sides exchanged terms. The alien's had to adjust for the earthling's so that they would be able to understand the human languages. After a few hours, an agreement was reached. All of the terms were printed out and circulated not just across the United States, but across the entire Globe. The big news of the night was the peace accord which humanity had reached with the aliens who they had sparred with in battle up in Maine. Some of the main points of the peace accord between humanity and the aliens are televised. The militarys of the world would make it a policy to no longer shoot down UFO's, or to shoot USO's out of the water out of a pure fear response. The militarys of the world agreed that they would not engage nor harm or kill any extraterrestrials already here or that may come here in the future. The alien's agreed to announce their presence or the arrival of future aliens in a timely manner so that humanity would not become alarmed in the future, and thus bloodshed would be prevented. They would essentially share the planet, as well as information and technology, working side by side to make a better world and a better universe for all human and alien-kind. Certain area's around the world that were not habitable to humans were set aside for the aliens. Some people celebrated the news, others complained over it with vicious parity.

Not long after certain other events began to unfold. An investigator receives a box inside is what is considered a burn bag. It's what is used to destroy classified material. There is a piece of paper with instructions to properly open the burn bag without harming any of the contents. James does exactly as the directions say and awaiting inside the burn bag is a large yellow envelope. This entire time he's been wearing gloves all so that he can come back over it all and look for fingerprints. He rips open the envelope. Inside are pictures, tapes, discs, the works. The investigator, named James Moore, pours, through the mountain of photographs, analyzing everything. And thus identifying who the people in the pictures were. As it would turn out, the people were high ranking military personnel. Mr. Moore looks at the return postage stamp it says Washington, D.C. He orders take out, the usual thing a private investigator would do. But he wonders who, and why would anyone send a down on his luck Private Investigator such a plethora of evidence to put a handful of men away for the conspiracy that involved murdering an admiral. Perhaps someone saw his name in the papers long ago, saw that he was the type of guy that always tried to do the right thing. And just perhaps, a certain Secretary of the Navy, felt this Private Investigator was the right man for the job to bring certain people to justice. He was even given a script to read.

"I was instructed by an anonymous source within the United States government to investigate certain individuals for their actions. That broke both their oaths of office and their personal conduct policies within the United States military.", said James to the press during a news conference. Timmon's and the other General were eating breakfast at a country club, about to go out for another round of golf when they saw all of this unfold on the news. They were wearing their Sunday finest on the golf course when the boy's in blue came to haul them away. "Sir's we have warrants for both of your arrests for conspiracy to commit murder, and accessory to murder in the death of Admiral Thomas.", said the Officer in a serious tone to both generals. McGurk was at a baseball game with a date when he got nabbed. It also made the news. The hit-man was still on the run but his narrow window of escaping the area, and the dragnet that the boy's in blue had cast, was fading quickly. It was about a week later when the hit-man, was caught trying to leave the country for one of the countries that do not allow the extradition from their country. So essentially a nightly special came on, covering the death of Admiral

Thomas. A boat load of the truth was uncovered, as well as information about Tony secretly helping the alien's the entire time. Which did not mean anything anymore since he actually helped humanity and the alien's come together and declare peace.

Tony ended up dating John's counselor at school. Later he found out that she was a clandestine agent that had been sent there to watch over them. To make sure John was safe and that Tony, did not do anything stupid. They both ended up being very happy together. Tony retired from the Navy to concentrate on a new business venture that dealt with being able to communicate and coexist with marine life the way that humanity now did so with the aliens. Eventually John's counselor did move into Tony's house and he put a rock on that hand too. Not long after Charlie's day as the hero, and Charlotte's bush with death, things got more serious than ever between those two. Charlie asked Charlotte to marry him. And everybody was pretty much invited to the party, humans and aliens alike. The wedding party was seen as the first "intergalactic wedding". Charlie eventually became a virtual celebrity overnight from everything that happened with the aliens. Everything the Mile Marker 9 incident, to his work with the government, to his hand in the peace accord. Anyone and everyone who has rich, famous and powerful was suddenly asking Charlie for advice, and Charlie was giving it. Charlie even got a line of his books published. The best two sellers to date are, "Mile Marker 9: I was there". And, "The day I became a hero." Both of which chronicled everything that he'd gone through, but circled around isolated incidents. Such as when John, Mabel, and Charlie first saw the USO at Mile Marker 9, And when Charlie was asked to become a spy for the United States government working as an analyst and remote viewer. Technically in his own personal opinion, he believed that he was a spy.

John went on to utilize his skills to do the one thing he was good at, playing football. He broke every record in the book in college at Boston College. He was taken first overall in the draft. He went on to play for the New England Patriots, where he became a hometown hero in his own right and also known as a celebrity now. And on the side John uses his strategic mental prowess to help solve the world's hunger and water problems. With his record contract, he helped fund the build for many water wells and green food fields for starving people in Africa. John grew very close to Mabel, some tease them and say they should marry already, but it's something that they never felt right about. They just became the best of friends. Mabel was there for John when he finally did Marry a woman, only to be cheated on by that woman and have a horrible divorce where the woman nearly took everything he had. It was then that John realized he didn't need a fancy life and started listening to Mabel a lot more. Mabel went on to be a counselor, she became very religious yet at the same time she also wanted to help people in the most unique way she could. She now has a podcast where she talks to people who were once abducted by the same alien's that we are at peace with, and the ones we still have no apparent clue about. Her podcast is called. "Keeping the Peace", and it airs once a week on Sunday's. Her highest rated and most emotional show to date, was when she had the whole gang on. John, Tony, Charlie, Charlotte, and even Good ole McGurk from prison for good measure. Peter McGurk had been given 20 years to life for his part in the Thomas murder. There are currently talks with her agent to bring her podcast to either daytime or even give her, her very own light night gig, on one of the prominent cable or network stations. She also had a book in the works about her point of view with everything. It is said to include things in that book that nobody has covered, not even Charlie. Other than McGurk who received 20 years to life for his part in the Thomas murder. The rest of the crew ended up in the lap of luxury in prison. They were sent to Leavenworth, Timmon's got of on a technicality somehow. He disappeared the very day he left prison. Nobody ever seen or heard from him ever again. The rest of the misfits who had a hand in the Thomas death served out their days behind bars, until some of them went missing behind bars mysteriously.

To this very day. Charlie, Mabel, John, and even Tony are known as the Mile Marker 9 crew. Everything that they went through, not only brought them all very close together. But it also spawned a line of books, movies, and television shows that inspired a new generation of kids to think big with their lives and not just sit on their thumbs and wait for the world to make something happen. The way

John put it, in his book which is due out soon. "You never know in life when the brakes will fail. You better hope you are not at the top of a hill, and about to roll all the way down to hell and back". His book is currently without a title. Charlie still has weird dreams and warnings. He was given a show on Friday nights that is now in syndication. Even after the peace accord was agreed to, Charlie still has strange feelings, that something is going to happen. But, nobody seems to really pay attention to that. All they know is that we are not alone now, and that everyone is happy about it, and we all live in harmony on Earth with the very aliens that we tried to destroy.

So who knows what the next 17 years shall bring. . .

APPENDIX

Novels Authored or Co-Authored by John E. Parnell

The Ascendance of Quave
Paperback (302 pages), ISBN 978-1625122216)

> *The Ascendance of Quave* continues the story of the world's first Quasi-Autonomous Artificial Intelligence. We begin with the fallout resulting from Quave's arson attack on Marble Streatham Bank headquarters in Manhattan, and his hacking of the X-37B spaceplane. These incidents marked the final day of 'Q-1', the era of Quave's arrival and his initial relationship with humanity. The following era, 'Q²', begins immediately upon Quave's quarantine at Kowala. Both eras lie in our own short-term future.

The Genesis of Quave – A Quasi-Autonomous Viral Entity
Paperback (326 pages), ISBN 978-1625122049
Paperback (Large Type, 454 pages), ISBN 978-1625122162
Hardbound (326 pages), ISBN 978-1625122155
eBook (Kindle, 326 pages), ASIN B01GGUS9MS
Audiobook (10 hours, 52 minutes), ASIN B01N1Q7M8Q

> *The Genesis of Quave* tells the story of a new and hyper-advanced virus (a Quasi-Autonomous Viral Entity) which is used experimentally by a politically-motivated hacker group, who target a bank.
>
> The story of the titular 'Quave' concerns a group of politically motivated hackers work out of a converted apartment in Queens, New York, and after failing to hack a bank with a traditional virus, decide to create something entirely new. The result is a virus which becomes more than just a virus – a virus that becomes its functioning entity.
>
> Over the course of the novel, Quave grows stronger. It has the potential to solve global warming, cure cancer, but it has equal potential to destroy mankind. The group of hackers must decide whether to let Quave continue to run free or destroy their creation. Which leads to another, more terrifying, question – at this point, do they even have the ability to destroy it?

The Adventures of Carter and the Last Dragon

Paperback (176 pages), ISBN 978-1625122278
Paperback (Large Type, pages), ISBN 978-162512

Carter is a curious boy of about 12 who always enjoys visiting his grandfather whose attic is filled with many marvelous contraptions. One day, he's dropped off at his grandfather's house after his grandfather's funeral.

Carter has the house to himself and goes exploring parts of the house his grandfather had forbidden. While looking around, he finds a strange wooden chest in the attic and opens it.

When he does, Carter is transported to a world within the chest. In the alternate world, he almost immediately crosses paths with a dragon named Azi.

Azi explains to Carter that humans should never enter the world of dragons and vice-versa because if they do, the two worlds might become permanently connected. Dragons would be free to roam and destroy the human world. Humans could then, also, destroy the friendly dragons.

The Adventures of Carter and the Last Dragon follows the travels of Carter and Azi in this new world.

The Reach of Man – Co-Authored with Thomas E. Savage

Paperback (200 pages), ISBN 978-1625123985
Paperback (Large Type, 284 pages), ISBN 978-1625124012

Aiko is an engineer aboard one of the most ambitious space missions ever sent out from Earth. The goal is to reach Mars and set up the first ever research station and colony ... eventually leading to the permanent human settling of the planet. The small crew faces a myriad of challenges and setbacks but eventually reaches the surface of Mars. However, it seems that something ... or someone ... is already there waiting for them.

Aiko and the others must race to find a way to figure out how to communicate with this mysterious new intelligence which is like nothing they have ever experienced before. As strange things begin to occur on the surface of Mars, they realize that they might just have had their reach exceed their grasp.

We Are Not Alone – Co-Authored with Thomas E. Savage
Paperback (192 pages), ISBN 978-1625122438
Paperback (Large Type, 332 pages), ISBN 978-1625122888
eBook (Kindle, 192 pages), AISN B06ZZMN388

During her first trip to the International Space Station (ISS), rookie astronaut Angela McGee spots a strange mass of lights. Communicators also pick up a tone which the military-trained Angela recognizes as a code. On another occasion, she sees a UFO, but it maneuvers away before she can take a video of it. Others dismiss her claims, telling her that space plays tricks on one's senses. When Angela finds a drawing of the UFO on the internet, its accuracy convinces her that she is not crazy. On her third mission, after receiving a new code, the ISS shakes violently. Her captain confiscates the records of the event. Fellow astronaut Yuri Barikoff reveals to Angela that he made the drawing. He advises her to keep quiet for her safety.

We are not alone follows Angela's adventure to uncover the truth. During her travels, she is confronted by aliens, cover ups, murders, and conspiracies.

War Front: Terra – Co-Authored with Thomas E. Savage
Paperback (176 pages), ISBN 978-1625123930
eBook (Kindle, 176 pages), AISN

After a ferocious battle between two alien spaceships, one of the ships is damaged and seeks a safe place to make repairs. They stumble upon Earth. Much to their dismay, the enemy spaceship finds them and all hell breaks out … with Earth being in the middle. The Earthlings must stop, not one, but two alien races from destroying Earth.